A *Candlelight*
Ecstasy Classic Romance

"WHAT RULES DO YOU PLAY THE GAME BY, COLBY?"

His kiss was not tentative, but gentle, wooing. Jase brought the kiss to an end slowly, delicately. "Does Matt play by your rules, Colby? Who is he to you? Tell me, Colby. Tell me."

It had taken her a moment to assimilate the deeply whispered sounds, but after they formed into coherent words, she came out of enchantment with a jolt. Colby landed a glancing blow to his shin. When he straightened up, she snarled, "Touch me and I'll give you another set of teeth marks to match the ones you already have." He didn't move toward her, so she continued heatedly. "The rules I play by, Jase Culhane, don't include seduction to gain information. Remember that ground rule. It might save your shins."

CANDLELIGHT ECSTASY CLASSIC ROMANCES

CANDLELIGHT ECSTASY ROMANCES®

THE CAPTIVE LOVE

Anne N. Reisser

A CANDLELIGHT ECSTASY CLASSIC ROMANCE

Published by
Dell Publishing Co., Inc.
1 Dag Hammarskjold Plaza
New York, New York 10017

Dell ® TM 681510, Dell Publishing Co., Inc.

A Candlelight Ecstasy Classic Romance

Candlelight Ecstasy Romance®, 1,203,540, is a registered trademark of Dell Publishing Co., Inc.

ISBN: 0-440-11059-9

Printed in the United States of America

One Previous Edition

March 1987

10 9 8 7 6 5 4 3 2 1

WFH

To Our Readers:

By popular demand we are happy to announce that we will be bringing you two Candlelight Ecstasy Classic Romances every month.

In the upcoming months your favorite authors and their earlier best-selling Candlelight Ecstasy Romances® will be available once again.

As always, we will continue to present the distinctive sensuous love stories that you have come to expect only from Ecstasy and also the very finest work from new authors of contemporary romantic fiction.

Your suggestions and comments are always welcome. Please write to us at the address below.

Sincerely,

The Editors
Candlelight Romances
1 Dag Hammarskjold Plaza
New York, New York 10017

CHAPTER ONE

She was going to be late. Colby finished applying the rest of her makeup and grimaced at the face in the mirror. "I look like a tart!" was her invariable conclusion. It went with the job, but she hated seeing her usual appearance metamorphose into that of a sultry charmer. Normally she looked less than her age of twenty-one, but no one could say that about the exotic creature so harshly limned in the bathroom mirror.

"At least I don't have to cake my eyelashes with mascara," she announced with satisfaction to the provocative image who drooped ridiculously long fans of dark eyelashes at her and pursed a full inviting mouth, moist with the dark rose lip gloss she had just applied. When she was younger, she had been teased so much about the length and silky darkness of the eyelashes shading her violet-blue eyes that at one time she had almost trimmed them in despair. She couldn't help it if they looked false—they grew that way!

She carefully slipped into the dress she was going to wear for tonight's performance. Usually she didn't dress in her stage costume until she reached the club. It was far too outré for street wear, but she wouldn't have time to call Matt if she didn't get ready now. She'd throw a light coat over her ensemble to hide it, or some man would be sure to accost her. The close-fitting lines and deep decolletage of the midnight-blue tapestry sheath gave her high-breasted figure a voluptuous appeal never apparent in the shirts and jeans that were her normal daytime wear.

She snatched up her purse and keys, pulled a light raincoat out of the closet, and practically ran from the apartment. Drat Matt and his cautious insistence on using pay phones when she contacted him. She always argued that, were she suspected sufficiently to warrant a tap on her phone, she would have been a cooked canary long ago. He was adamant, however, so she dutifully drove to a pay phone on California and dropped the money in the slot.

She was hot, swathed in the raincoat, so she opened the door of the booth to let in a little air. It also turned off the light and gave her a bit of anonymity. She'd felt as she did when the spotlight picked her out on stage, impaled by the finger of light, cynosure of all those staring, avid eyes. She hated it! But, she mused wryly, it was necessary and she'd do it until the job was done. What was at stake was too important for her maidenly qualms of personal modesty to interfere. When this job was done, she could wear nothing but high-necked blouses for the rest of her life if she wanted to!

"Narcotics Division, Carter speaking," crackled the voice issuing crisply from the receiver she held in her hand.

"Lieutenant MacGuire, please, Dave. Colby here."

"He's on another line, Colby. Can you hold for a sec?"

"Okay, Dave, but I'm running late. I've just got time to make it to the club. John Barnes hyperventilates whenever he thinks I'm going to be late for a performance. Can you brief me or do I have to wait for Matt?"

"He wants to talk to you, Colby. I'll tell him you're on the line and he'll be right with you."

Colby drummed her fingers on the shelf in the phone booth. Suddenly she was uneasy. She felt too exposed and the hairs on the nape of her neck rose in prickling awareness. Someone was watching her. She scanned the shadowed street anxiously but saw nothing untoward. What foot traffic there was hurried about its own legitimate business, and the cars parked within her range of vision seemed empty. The evening fog overhead was rolling down a light blanket to tuck San Francisco in for the night, and the streetlights were fluttering and flickering to life.

Reassured by the stillness around her, she muttered, "Just nerves. Dave sounded portentous. You're just reacting to that, Colby."

"Is someone with you, Colby?" Matt's voice sounded sharply in her ear.

"Oh, hi, Matt." She hadn't realized she was now off hold. "I'm in a booth on California. I was just talking to myself. A sudden attack of prickly nape and I was talking myself out of it."

"Are you sure no one's watching you?" Matt's voice was anxious. He was uneasy about allowing Colby to have any part of this anyway and it made him oversensitive.

Oh, blast! Colby thought sourly. *Now I've done it. Matt's going into an avuncular attack, having qualms about letting me work for him, and I'll have to waste time soothing him.*

"I'm sure, Matt. Just a quick case of the heebie-jeebies. It's gone now and I'm really running late. You know John Barnes . . . we don't want his ulcer flaring."

"This is a critical time, Colby, a very dangerous time,

11

in fact. Are you sure you want to go on with it? Just say the word and we'll pull you out . . . in fact, maybe I should anyway. If anything went wrong and something happened to you, I'd never forgive myself."

Colby leaned against the wall of the phone booth, thoughtfully pulling at her lower lip and shaking her head in exasperation. The soft fall of inky black hair belled out away from the receiver she had pressed to her ear. For a ruthless, tough police lieutenant, Matthew MacGuire was sounding more and more like a maiden aunt every day.

"My maiden aunt!" She spoke her thoughts aloud. Matthew's subordinates would have had a stroke collectively to have heard her address him thusly, but he only chuckled. "At the risk of repeating myself ad nauseam, Matt, we've had all this out before when I came to you and offered to work undercover for you. I knew the risks, but if I *must* descend to platitudes—'The game is worth the candle.' I run much less risk than one of your regular people would. I've certainly got a legitimate talent, and that gives me a good cover at the club. Who's going to suspect the spoiled little rich girl rebelling against the tyrannical father? I sing in a popular dive that caters to all the other rebelling rich kids. I don't sing like a narc and I don't look like a narc and there's just enough truth, obvious to those who care to look, to support my cover. My father has loudly made his opinion of my job clear to all. I don't think Barnes has recovered yet from the tongue-lashing Father gave him when he came to my show.

"Speaking of dear old Daddy, has he made any headway with the-powers-that-be in getting the club license revoked? Or were you able to squash that charming little gambit of his?"

12

"I didn't have to," Matt admitted through gritted teeth. "Strings, from sources we will not mention, were pulled. It seems you are valuable to the 'owners,' silent and otherwise, of the club. You draw in the clientele they're after—like you said, all the rebelling rich kids. Otherwise you'd have been sent packing when Daddy started raising the dust. Our silent friends do not like the attention of the police being drawn to any of their activities."

"Exactly," she said with smug satisfaction. "They need me and you need me, and soon we'll close down that club permanently, Matt. When Sandi died from a drug overdose, I swore I'd do my damnedest to get the swine who hooked her on the stuff. She was my best friend, my roommate at boarding school for five years, and someone's going to pay for her death. Poor little rich kids have as many problems as any other human beings, and too many of my friends have taken a start down a road that will take them Sandi's way, thanks to the people who hide in the shadows of that club."

"I know," he sighed into the phone. Colby could picture him running a hand wearily around the back of his beefy bull neck and exasperatedly rumpling his gray hair. It was a characteristic gesture when he wasn't getting his own way, which, to be fair, didn't happen too often. Just mostly with Colby. Born stubborn, she'd had twenty-one years of practice to refine the art.

"Matt, was there anything at all special? I'm really late and—"

"And you'll expect me to fix any speeding tickets you get if you're held up any longer. Okay, Colby. Word is out that a big shipment is due in at the end of the month. If we can pinpoint the delivery date, we can catch even the big sharks in the net this time. You've seen pictures of

D'Angelo and Stark. If either of them shows up at the club within the next three days, it'll go a long way toward confirming the information we have so far. Keep your eyes open for them and everything else that might point to where and when, but for God's sake, be careful! Reconstructive surgery is wonderful, but I don't think even it could put that beautiful face and body of yours back together if those boys get wind of who you are and what you're up to." Now Matt's voice was deadly serious and Colby shivered slightly.

"I know, Matt. I'll be careful. I promise." Her words were heartfelt and he accepted them, grudgingly allowing her to close the conversation.

She left the shelter of the phone booth and walked quickly toward her waiting car. Her long legs flashed in the light and the click of her high heels beat out a staccato rhythm on the pavement. The slope of the San Francisco hill pulled against the muscles in her calves. When the two men loomed unexpectedly in front of her, her breath choked in her throat. It flashed through her mind that of all the dangers she had considered when she chose her present course, mugging had completely escaped her list. Would Matt say "I told you so"?

On the theory that a good, lung-filling scream is worth a thousand karate tricks, of which she knew not a one anyway, she sucked in a deep breath and opened her mouth, only to release the breath on a relieved gasp.

"Oh, Davis, you scared hell out of me, popping up in front of me that way! I nearly screamed and got you arrested for an attempted mugging."

The two men who fronted her were suave and business-suited. Their only muggings would be of the financial kind, for the stock market and the boardrooms were their natural habitats. Honestly, Matt was going to make a nervous wreck of her. If his dire warnings hadn't still been ringing in her head, she would never have panicked like that.

"Your father wants to see you, Miss Colby," spoke the taller of the two men. He was her father's personal secretary. She didn't recognize the other man, but he was sure to be some errand boy of her father's.

"Father will just have to wait, Davis," she said calmly, and even in the dimming light she could see the shocked expressions on the faces of the two men. No one, not even his only daughter, asked Steven Duncan to wait. People waited for him, not the other way around.

Colby continued with exaggerated patience that masked a will as strong as her father's. It had caused many a notable explosion between them. "I have a job, Davis. A job for which I get paid a salary and for which I have great hopes." If her lips twisted wryly at these last words, the two men watching her could be forgiven for misreading the cause of her irony.

Steven Duncan's daughter could live a life of pampered social ease, smothered in luxury, every wish instantly granted. Every wish, that is, except for the one that would grant her a father who took the time to see his daughter as a person rather than an asset to manipulate. More than once Steven Duncan had sought to use Colby's undeniable beauty as the mortar that would bind a business merger and had got his ears figuratively, if not literally, pinned back. They were more respectful antagonists than father and daughter. There was a wary respect between them as well as an exasperated affection, but as Colby had reminded her father on more than one occasion, filial duty went just so far. It did not extend to marrying to please him.

When Steven had pressed her excessively on behalf of one particularly desirable suitor, desirable from a business standpoint, that is, she informed him that since he wasn't the one who was going to have to go to bed with that particular young man on the wedding night he would jolly well keep his nose out of her marital arrangements or lack of them. Steven, surprisingly, had laughed uproariously, conceded the point, and then found other means to conclude his business deal.

The conflict was understandable. Colby was herself the product of what might have been termed a *mariage de convenance* between two powerful business interests, and while it had never been a grand passion, it suited her parents. Therefore her father saw nothing strange in desiring a similar arrangement for his only daughter. She would have wealth, an attentive husband—any man would be attentive to *her*—and it wasn't as if he were asking her to marry some disgusting man old enough to be her grandfather, for heaven's sake!

Colby assured him she saw his point, but still declined firmly. When the time came, she'd pick her own husband, thank you very much, and he wouldn't be part of a package deal.

When she left school and got a job as a singer in the less than salubrious environs of a North Beach nightclub that catered to a young, but not unwashed, clientele, many of whom were friends and acquaintances of Colby's, clashes between Colby and her father had increased in frequency and severity. The last one had resounded throughout the Montgomery Street offices of Duncan Associates and was still a subject for discussion among all subordinates, down to the lowliest junior mail clerk.

The quarrel had caused Steven's ulcer to flare again and

his ensuing misery was in no way mitigated by his daughter's acerbic comments anent his threat to cut off her funds. She informed him she could live most comfortably on her own earnings and proceeded to do so by simply making no more withdrawals from the checking account that serviced her quarterly checks from the trust fund established for her upon her grandmother's death when Colby was fifteen.

If her father could justly be described as having a will of iron, then Colby's might, by definition, be called a will of steel, and fire-tempered steel at that. She was black Irish through her mother's side and never was the strain stronger. For all her femininity she had the Celtic gift of invective as well.

All this the men who faced the slender, disdainful figure knew well, and it made their job no easier. But they had their orders and were prepared to carry them out, even at the substantial risk to their life and limb, including their ears.

"Miss Colby, that's all taken care of," the man she called Davis said soothingly. "Your father has to fly to Europe unexpectedly and he wants to see you before he goes."

"Why?" Her tone was more than suspicious. It was frankly disbelieving and hostile.

Davis shrugged with what he hoped conveyed masterly ignorance. "I only work for Mr. Duncan, Miss Colby. He says 'Do' or 'Go' and I do or go. He doesn't say why to me."

Slightly mollified, Colby acknowledged the truth of that statement. "No, explanations have never been my father's strong suit," she agreed ruefully. "Well, Davis, be that as it may, I still have some songs to sing at the club. I'll go

17

to the airport after my first show. When does his flight leave?"

The man next to Davis shifted restlessly and Colby's eyes snapped toward him. They couldn't see her eyebrow quirk in the dim light, but it was a mannerism familiar to all of Steven Duncan's employees, and in him it usually presaged explosive activity, either verbal or physical, depending on circumstances.

Davis understood the gathering tension in the set of her shoulders and the instinctive half step backward she took when Motham had moved toward her slightly. He glared at his companion. This was Steven Duncan's daughter and it would be worth both their jobs if she didn't keep her appointment at the airport. If Motham startled or spooked her, she'd be off like a scalded cat, and he knew all too well that she'd cause a scene with no compunction whatsoever if she chose, and she sure would choose if they tried to haul her to the airport against her will.

"He leaves very soon, Miss Colby," he assured her, placatory and calming. "On his orders we obtained a replacement for you for tonight. The management was most obliging; you're released from both your shows." He smiled hopefully at her.

"I'll just bet they were obliging," she spat bitterly. "Steven Duncan's money can buy a lot of obliging. Well, Davis, you'll understand if I check with the club management before I go out to the airport. My dear father wouldn't be above trying to lose me a job through default of contract by nonappearance if it suited one of his twisty plans. If the management has consented and the substitute is agreeable to them for tonight, I'll see dear Daddy." Her manner bode ill for dear Daddy, and Davis winced. Motham, never having witnessed a clash between sire and offspring, stood happily by in blissful ignorance.

She wheeled with supple grace and headed back toward the phone booth. Motham, silent until now, moved after her involuntarily, stopping only when Davis grasped his arm and hauled him to a stop.

"Relax," he ordered sharply. "It's all been covered. Steven Duncan's plans are always thorough and she'll only find that she's been replaced for this one night. Tomorrow, after she's well on her way, the club will be told that the replacement will be permanent."

Colby fumed as she strode back to the phone booth. How like her father to arrogantly rearrange any and all plans others made in order to suit his own convenience. He should have learned through hard experience that she was no tame cat to leap through his hoops. Whatever plans he was fomenting now were going to get short shrift from her, and that she would make most clear to him, face-to-face, at the airport. She slammed into the phone booth and rattled coins down the slot.

As she expected, she found indeed that an adequate replacement had been signed in to cover for her tonight. John Barnes wasn't particularly pleased to have his routine disrupted, especially on such short notice, but as she had surmised, Steven Duncan could buy a lot of obliging. Besides, Barnes wasn't too anxious to have another run-in with a man of Duncan's caliber. The last one was still painfully fresh in his memory. Steven Duncan placated was infinitely desirable to Steven Duncan irascible, even at the cost of some disruption to the smooth running of his club. Colby was very popular, and her replacement would have an uphill struggle.

"I'm sorry, Mr. Barnes. I had no idea that my father

was going to do something like this. Evidently he's going to Europe tonight and urgently needs to see me. I'll do my best to be back for the second show." Colby soothed outwardly, even if she seethed inwardly.

By the time she hung up, Barnes was calmer, especially since he knew that in all probability she'd be there for the second show, which was when the rowdier element would be present. Colby's presence at that show would defuse incipient trouble. For her part, Colby was determined to be back for the second show. Matt would be counting on her to be there, ready to spot D'Angelo or Stark, should they make an appearance. She always wandered through the tables during her act so she could look for them unobtrusively. If she found one or both of them, she might even sit in their laps! Matt would have a conniption fit, she grinned mischievously.

She was still smiling slightly at the thought as she went back to the two waiting men, but her smile died swiftly as the reality of the situation came back to her. "All right," she said curtly. "I talked to Barnes and I'm covered. What airline is Father taking this time, and where am I to meet him?"

"We'll drive you, Miss Colby," offered Davis smoothly. "He'll be in a private room. You know how he hates crowds. I'll have to lead you to him."

"All right," Colby agreed ungraciously. "You can lead me to him, but I'll take my own car. I'll follow you out to the airport. I want my own transport, since I don't plan to hang around after I've heard what dear Daddy has to say."

Without waiting, taking their agreement for granted— Colby had her own share of arrogant assurance—she headed for her car. She missed the abortive move Motham made for her, for it was again forestalled by Davis.

"Knock it off, you idiot!" Davis hissed. "Do you want to ruin everything?"

"Well, we ought to take her in the car with us. What if she decides not to follow us out there after all?" Motham excused himself sulkily.

"She will," Davis assured him. "She's madder than hops at Daddy and is just itching to tear a strip or two off of him. She'll follow us, all right, right on our rear bumper, unless I miss my guess, fuming all the way."

"Tear a strip off of Steven Duncan?" repeated Motham weakly. He looked at the slender girl getting into her car with considerably more respect than he had shown before.

"I've seen her chew pieces off of his ears when she really gets going," Davis assured him. "She's Steven Duncan's daughter, all right, for all that she takes after her mother's side of the family in looks. Why do you think Duncan is going to such lengths now? Any other girl in her position would be happy to live the life Duncan offered her. She could be traveling all over the world right now, skiing in Austria in the winter, lounging in Hawaii. You name it, Duncan would see that she got to do it, and where is she? Singing in some dive and being ogled by a bunch of drunks."

"Well, she's got an awfully good voice," offered Motham, as though he felt it incumbent upon him to offer some excuse for an obvious insanity on Colby's part.

"Of course she's got a good voice! She's got a sexy-as-hell voice!" Davis snorted. "Duncan would see that she got a recording contract if she'd let him. The girl's got star quality and tremendous stage presence, and Steven Duncan would be happy to see her a household word, if it got her out of that club." The two men got into their own car and Davis started the drive to the airport. He continued instructing the other man. "That was one of the times she shredded his ears. He offered to start a record company for her or buy into a recognized one if she insisted on having a career. She said No once, politely, and when he kept pressing the issue, she lost her temper, and believe me, she has a lot of temper to lose. I thought his ulcer was going to kick loose and finally hemorrhage. He was eating Maalox tablets like they were candy when she got finished. So was I."

"Wow" was all the other man could whisper reverently.

"Wow indeed," agreed Davis and drove a little faster.

Colby sped up too. She wasn't riding his bumper—she was too good a driver for that—but no car had a chance to cut in between them. The more she thought about it, the smellier it got. Her father was definitely up to something, otherwise why drag her all the way out to the airport? Phones had been invented a long time ago and she had been home all afternoon except for fifteen minutes or so when she ran out to borrow some milk to go in her coffee. If he had tried to call her during that time and missed her, he had plenty of secretaries who could spend the afternoon dialing until their fingers were worn to nubs (except that all the phones had punch buttons now, but the principle was the same) and one of them was bound to have caught her. Nope, she was supposed to go to the airport for some reason.

Suddenly she chuckled. What if her father wanted to trot out some new prospect in the matrimonial stakes? What a shock it would be for her father when she turned up in her costume and stage makeup. She had no illusions about her appearance. In this getup, sweet and innocent she was not! More like "I've seen it all," but then that was the image her act was supposed to project. To anyone who knew her really well, it was a subtle burlesque, being totally foreign to Colby's true nature. Jeans, shirts, and scrubbed, makeup-free face were her normal wont, but, true to her nature, when she did a job, she did it thoroughly. To those she was in contact with at the club, she was a world-weary rich girl, out for kicks and a new thrill, and her singing job was just another prick against her rich father. Her life might depend on the believability of her portrayal of her role, so she made sure it was believable.

She could tell that Davis had wanted to suggest that she change before they went to the airport. It had been obvious in the subdued dismay every time he looked at her, but he hadn't quite dared to press his luck. Anyway, she wouldn't have agreed since she intended to go directly back to the club after she and Daddy had had their little chat.

She accelerated smoothly as the cars funneled onto the Bayshore Freeway and edged the car that was trying to slip into line between Davis and herself smartly back into its own lane. The driver shot her a furious glare that changed ludicrously when he got a good look at her. He smiled ingratiatingly and mouthed, "What's your phone number, honey?" She froze him with an icy stare and concentrated on her driving. She might have to take that at the club, but not on the freeway, in the privacy of her own car.

Davis flicked on his turn signal as the airport exit loomed ahead and she dutifully followed suit. He didn't head for the central parking garage, but wound instead through some back ways to a small, dimly lit area away from the main terminals. He parked the car and Colby pulled into a slot beside his car.

The two men got out and flanked her as they all moved toward a doorway that had a light burning over it. It was very quiet and deserted and Colby felt a niggling disquiet. There were nothing but smaller aircraft parked in this area, though there were several executive jets as well. She didn't think any of them had enough range to get across the Atlantic, let alone Germany, which was where her father was probably going. She knew he was working on a minimerger with a German electronics firm. *Maybe he has a German* Graf *lined up for me,* she thought sardonically. *Money and a title. Would I be a* Graffess? *No, that's not right. A* Grafen? *Well, whatever. . . . I'll bet I could make him pop his monocle, click his heels, and run for the hills.* Cheered by these reflections she went docilely into the door Davis held open for her and looked around, expecting to see her father.

It was a rather bare room, in all probability some sort of briefing room. It had as its main items of furniture a Formica-topped table, some uncomfortable-looking folding chairs, and a not-too-well-erased blackboard with some squiggly diagrams only half obliterated.

Her father wasn't present. In fact the only other occupant besides herself and her two escorts was a lounging figure in high-heeled cowboy boots, tight and rather dusty blue jeans, and a faded checked Western-style shirt that was rolled up above his elbows.

He had been leaning lazily against the edge of the table when they came in, arms folded casually across his chest. As Davis closed the door behind them, he, whoever he was, stood slowly but lithely upright and hooked his thumbs in the belt loops of his low-slung jeans. He looked

Colby up and down once and his opinion was written clearly enough across his face to make a hectic flush stain her cheeks. Her eyes narrowed dangerously and she gave him back stare for stare.

I'm not going to like you, mister, she thought to herself. *It's a good thing you're not going to be my problem.* He was a good-looking brute, shining cap of hair as blue-black as her own, but where her eyes were a melting violet-blue, except when she was angry and they darkened to a night-storm blue, his were a strange silvery gray, contrasting strongly against the bronze of his skin.

He was big, six foot two or three, she estimated, and had shoulders to match. A mean customer in a fight was her conclusion, lean-hipped, with a deep-muscled chest and forearms brawny enough for a stevedore. Those boots weren't for show. They were riding boots, well worn, with a narrow tapered heel. She had become very observant recently. Her life now depended on it, as did the success of her self-imposed mission. There was even a tang of horse and open space about him—the room was small and slightly overheated. Conclusion: a working cowboy. What was he doing here in the big city, and where was her father?

"Where's my father, Davis?" she asked sharply.

"I imagine he's home, Miss Colby," Davis answered her smoothly.

Colby's mind worked furiously but she didn't have enough information. It was too elaborate for the owners of the club. If they'd wanted to get rid of her, a hit-and-run accident was easy to stage. Ergo, still her father's plot.

"Why is my father at home, Davis?" she questioned him gently, using the tone one might use to the mentally deficient, spacing and subtly emphasizing each syllable.

Davis flushed and Motham began to see what Davis meant. He felt a sneaking sympathy grow unbidden for Duncan. Perhaps being rich wasn't all beer and skittles if one had a daughter like this one.

Davis didn't answer Colby directly. "Has her luggage been delivered?" He directed his question to the cowboy, who was now lounging against the table. He'd evidently decided that she wasn't lady enough to warrant the courtesy of standing while she still stood, Colby fumed.

"It's being stowed in my plane now," the cowboy answered laconically. His voice was deep and slightly drawling but there was a precision to his pronunciation that had a faintly Eastern flavor, a lingering crispness perhaps. Educated and cultured was Colby's sudden conviction, and there was an air of command and authority about him in spite of his casual pose.

She looked closely at his hands, still hooked negligently at his waist. They were long-fingered and sinewy, but the nails were close-trimmed and spotless. Strong, capable hands, hands that could control a plunging mount or gentle a woman's body. Now, why in heaven's name had that idiotic thought flashed through her brain?

She turned her attention back to Davis. She noted that he and Motham were between her and the only door in the room, and something in their stances said they meant to stay that way.

"My luggage, Davis?" she asked him purringly. "Is it *my* luggage that's being loaded somewhere, Davis?"

Davis gulped. All of a sudden he wasn't sure that the salary Steven Duncan paid him was really enough. He didn't like the look in Colby's eyes. No wonder Steven Duncan had an ulcer. Even with all that makeup on she was beautiful, but right now he wouldn't give a plugged nickel for his chances if she met him in a dark alley. She looked like she'd slide a knife between his ribs and walk away whistling, with never a backward look.

"Yes, it's your luggage, Miss Duncan." The confirmation was made by that deep-measured voice behind her, and Colby turned back to look at the man who was now standing upright again. He'd even taken his thumbs out of his belt loops and his folded fists rested on his hips.

"I'm going somewhere," Colby stated with what seemed like detached interest.

"You are," that voice drawled, little threads of mockery weaving in and out of the short syllables.

"With you."

"With me."

"Where?"

The individual words were getting choppier and more clipped. She felt, rather than heard, the two men behind her shift uncomfortably, but all her attention was fixed on the silvery gray eyes that bored into hers so relentlessly.

"To my ranch. Your father feels you've been playing too hard. All those late hours are bad for your youthful complexion, and he thinks some clean country air might restore the roses to your cheeks. We're very isolated and we have lots of clean air."

Not a flicker of a smile crossed his face, but she reacted to the mocking amusement deep in his eyes. Damn him and damn her father. They were about to ruin months of work, hers and Matt's, all unknowingly. And Matt! Matt would be frantic if she disappeared. He might tear the club apart looking for traces of her if she disappeared without a word. He'd immediately suspect the worst and he'd wreck the painstaking case they had all labored so hard on. She had to get away, somehow, some way.

There was a crackling tension in the small room. The three men watched the slender girl as she assimilated her position. She couldn't overpower three men all by herself, and Davis (she'd fix *him* when she got the chance) and that creep, whatever his name was, looked planted in front of the door.

"Davis," she informed him dangerously, "this is kidnapping. Don't think I won't make you and Father pay for it. If you go through with this, I'll make you wish you'd never been born. You have no idea what's at stake!"

"I take my orders from your father, Miss Colby." Davis was sweating lightly now. Duncan definitely didn't pay him enough.

"Well, *I* don't take orders from my father, Davis, and I'm going to walk out of here right now. If you lay a hand on me, I'll see you booked for assault and battery, and don't think it's an idle threat." She glared at the equally uncomfortable Motham. "And that goes for you too, Mr. Whatever-your-name-is. Ask Davis if you think I'm bluffing. He knows. I'm not Steven Duncan's daughter for nothing and I don't make threats I'm not prepared to carry out."

She saw it in Davis's eyes first. He wouldn't lay a hand on her if she went out of the door. She'd convinced him, and Motham would follow suit, taking his lead from Davis. She'd better get the hell out before they changed their minds. She didn't even think about the man behind her. He'd probably just been hired as the pilot or something. It'd be nothing to him if she stayed or went. Davis would see that he got paid for his time and trouble. Her father was always scrupulously fair about that, even in the matter of attempted kidnap of his own daughter. She didn't even look behind her as she advanced on the two men, who showed signs of moving back out of her way with indecent haste.

She had her hand on the doorknob when she heard an incredulous voice close behind her and felt a muscular arm loop around her waist and yank her backward. "You're going to let a spoiled brat of a daughter bluff you out? I didn't realize Steven Duncan had worms working for him. My plane's fueled and her luggage will be aboard by now. Let's get her on it before she reduces you two quivering blobs of Jell-O any further." His voice fanned her ear and the arm didn't loosen a fraction of its pressure. "I'll lay a hand on you, Miss Duncan, on the seat of your tight little dress, if you struggle or scream. Your father requested that I give you a little vacation at my home, and a vacation you'll have. I'm inclined to agree with him that you've been hanging around with the wrong sort of people and it's time to see what a little soap and water and regular hours will do for your disposition."

"Jase, are you sure . . . ?" Davis began uncertainly.

"I'm sure. Let's get going. Any messages for your father, Miss Duncan? Davis will be happy to pass them along for you." There was no subtlety in his sarcasm.

"Let me make a phone call and I'll give him the message directly," Colby snarled. "Let go of me, you spavined, cross-eyed offspring of a . . . oof." The breath rushed out of Colby's lungs as his arm contracted sharply, cutting off her words in midspate.

"Ah, ah!" he admonished her. "Watch your language, young miss. It's just possible that your tongue will require washing as well as your face. I have a young boy in my house and I don't want him picking up any big-city ways from you. We'll have a talk about all that later. Right now, you're to walk out to my plane by my side, and if you kick

29

up a fuss or try to run, I'll sling you over my shoulder. It's a very uncomfortable and undignified way to ride, I assure you, and there's not so much of you that I can't carry you like that for as long as I have to."

He removed his arm from around her midriff and grasped her wrist firmly. Colby rubbed her diaphragm with her free hand and glared up at him resentfully. She had a long way up to glare and she was no tiny morsel herself.

"I'll make you sorry for this. I promise you, if it's the last thing I ever do, I'll make you sorry. I don't know how much my father is paying you, but it won't be enough. I have my own friends and they're ones even my father can't handle. I told Davis"—she spared a contemptuous look over at him—"that he had no idea what's at stake and I'll repeat it to you. This is between my father and myself, and anyone who's unlucky enough to get caught in the middle is liable to get ground into very fine powder."

He seemed to find her amusing. Amazingly he smiled with something akin to enjoyment. Colby didn't realize that in spite of her makeup and dress at that moment she resembled nothing more than a tiny furious kitten, ready to take on the world for its catnip mouse. He just couldn't take her seriously for all her scathing words and he discounted them as thwarted bravado.

Davis knew better, but he wisely kept a still tongue in his head. Right now Colby was turning her ire on Jase and he was more her fighting weight. In his own way he was as formidable an opponent as Steven Duncan.

Davis knew that there was something more to this whole thing besides Duncan's dislike of Colby's singing job. Duncan had been unusually adamant that Colby had to be taken away from the club right now. Had she fallen for someone really disreputable? Davis wondered suddenly. Fight and disagree though they did, Steven Duncan really did love his daughter and would go to some lengths to keep her from getting hurt. She'd rejected all the eligible suitors Duncan had laid in her path with a rather insulting disdain, but that didn't mean she wasn't capable of finding someone more to her taste. Even with the getup she had on adding years to her true age, she was beautiful and she could be charming when she wasn't losing her temper. He'd usually seen her in a temper because that was the only time she came to beard her father in his office, but he had seen her at social gatherings on occasion and she was breathtakingly lovely.

"We've got a long way to fly," Jase drawled. "You can tell me all about what you and your friends will do to me when we get to my ranch. We'll have plenty of time for long conversations, Miss Duncan. You'll be with us for a while."

"Just how long do you intend to keep me?" she asked.

"Until your father lets me know that he doesn't want you to enjoy my hospitality anymore," he answered her smoothly and vaguely. "And now, enough delaying tactics. I've had a long day already, Miss Duncan, and it'll be a longer night."

He opened the door and, with his hand still clamped firmly around her wrist, pulled her after him out into the corridor. The two men trailed silently behind the lead pair as Jase took them further down the corridor and made a sharp right. After traversing several more corridors, he led them back outside. A plane stood waiting, its door invitingly open.

There wasn't another soul in sight and the just-short-of-circulation-cutting grip on her wrist hadn't eased a fraction. If she'd seen anyone, she would have screamed, Jase or no. A disturbance, allied with the fact that her car would be found at the airport, might have given Matt a valuable clue. The federal authorities were in on this investigation, and Matt would have no hesitation in calling on their resources when he found her gone. They'd check every flight, private and commercial, if there was anything to link her to this airport.

Just before Jase bundled her up the steps into the plane, Motham cleared his throat and said hesitantly, "What about her car?" She could have dropped him on the spot.

"Her car?" Jase asked.

"Er, yes," Davis explained. "She wouldn't ride with us. She drove her own car and it's parked out beside ours."

"Give the gentlemen the key to your car, Miss Duncan," Jase instructed her with heavy patience.

She sullenly complied. Jase had to release her wrist so that she could delve into her purse, but he stood so close that she knew he'd grab her at the first sign of flight. She might have chanced it if she were dressed in jeans and sneakers, but in heels and this damned tight dress, he'd catch her before she got ten feet.

She unhooked the car key from the leather folder holding all her keys and laid it silently in Davis's outstretched palm. He thrust it into his pants pocket and reassured her, "We'll leave the car in your parking slot at your apartment, Miss Colby. I'll leave the key at your father's office for safe keeping."

"Why not just use the key whoever packed my things used and leave it in the apartment, Davis? I'm evidently to have no privacy of any sort," Colby suggested with acid sweetness. "There's liquor in the cabinet over the range and plenty of food in the refrigerator. Just make yourself at home and don't leave dirty dishes in the sink!"

Davis had the grace to flush, and the hot dark red was evident even in the shadowy light of the taxi area. With that parting shot Colby mounted the steps into the airplane as an aristocrat during the Terror might have mounted the steps to the guillotine. Jase paused for a moment of low-voiced consultation with the two men by the foot of the stairs, but before Colby had time to explore her surroundings with more than a cursory glance, he followed her into the plane and dogged the hatch shut behind him.

"Go through to the cockpit and take the right seat. I want you where I can keep an eye on you in flight," he ordered.

"Afraid I might parachute out while your back is turned?" she gibed.

He looked at her defiant figure speculatively. "You know, I think you just might try it if you thought you could get away with it. You, Miss Duncan," he announced with the air of one making a surprising discovery, "are the most pigheaded woman and spoiled brat it has ever been my misfortune to run up against."

Colby's smile was maliciously saccharine. "Why, thank you, Jase. That's a compliment I'll treasure all my life. I'll do my best to live up to your expectations because I can see you're a man who enjoys being right. Far be it from me to prove you wrong in any respect."

She shrugged out of her raincoat and tossed it on one of the passenger seats, followed by her purse. She didn't seem to hear Jase's muffled intake of breath as the full impact of her costume hit him, but when she turned to make her way up the aisle toward the cockpit door, there was perhaps just the slightest bit of extra swing to the motion in her hips. It might have been due to the slight incline of the aisle, but whatever caused it, Jase's eyes were unwillingly appreciative as he watched her progress.

Colby slid into the copilot's seat and began to buckle herself in. She kicked off her shoes and shoved them back underneath the seat. Might as well be as comfortable as possible. As Jase had said, it was going to be a long night. She couldn't do anything about getting away right now, but perhaps, if she stayed alert, an opportunity would come when they arrived wherever they were going.

She wasn't going to make it easy for Jase Whoever-he-was. Between them, he and her father might find that they'd bitten off more than they could chew without choking. She planned to be a bone in the throat of this arrogant cowboy who thought kidnapping Colby Duncan was going to be a cinch job.

The cowboy might not realize it, but he was under a considerable handicap from the start. He couldn't hurt her, her father wouldn't stand for it, and she herself would have no compunction about laying him out with a handy two-by-four if the opportunity offered itself tonight.

Realistically speaking, however, she didn't think there was much chance of that. Those silver-gray eyes were altogether too keen and that muscular body too formidable to make him anything but a nasty customer in a fight, and she'd bet he'd been in a few in his time. There was something about the set of his shoulders that told her he was no stranger to physical confrontation. Several of the officers in Matt's department had the same aura. They were usually his best operatives. She sighed mentally. Her father had chosen her jailer well.

CHAPTER TWO

Colby tried her best to elicit some useful information from Jase during that long flight. She didn't even know where his ranch was, and he didn't seem in a hurry to enlighten her. Since it was a night of no moon, she wasn't even sure in what direction they were flying. She probed and prodded a little, but he only informed her bluntly, "My ranch is very isolated, Miss Duncan."

The subtle intonation he always laid on the "Miss" set Colby's teeth on edge. It tempted her to adopt a lady-of-the-manor inflection when she addressed him by his first name. If she had known his last name, she'd have called him by it without the "Mister" appended, she fumed.

There had been servants in her parents' homes but they had always been treated with dignity. For all his faults, Steven Duncan was no snob. He respected a man who did his job well, whatever that job might be. Colby had been raised in that tradition. To her, self-respect was an inner attribute that had little to do with outer circumstances and wealth, or lack of it. Her father would not have phrased it precisely that way, for to him wealth was a source of power and as such to be valued, but he could at least understand Colby's viewpoint, even when not totally in accord with it or the results thereof. He admired his daughter's pervasive sense of independence even while he sought to quell it or bend it to his own ends.

Colby had, however, observed others and their manner toward those subservient, and should she desire, could lay tongue to the exact, subtle shadings of voice that denigrate and lower self-esteem.

Not that she'd be able to dent this Jase's self-esteem! It was obviously at an all-time high, and nothing she could do at present was going to change that. A hard smile bent the corners of her mouth. That wasn't to say she would never be able to dent it. She wistfully visualized a sturdy two-by-four.

Jase was watching her out of the corner of his eye. He wondered what had brought out that strange, savage smile. Suddenly he also wondered just how candid Steven Duncan had been with him. This girl was a puzzle. He hadn't expected her to react so violently to her abduction. He expected her to be upset, yes. Her father had warned him that she was seventeen, spoiled, and uncontrollable. Duncan had also said that Colby's closest friend had recently died from a drug overdose and he'd be damned if he saw his own daughter go the same way. A girl of her type wouldn't be at all pleased to be immured indefinitely in the wilds, away from town pleasures, but she had been more than upset. She had been coldly furious.

And the way she'd faced down Davis. The man had been panic-stricken when she threatened him. Davis had actually chosen to go against Steven Duncan's direct and explicit orders. He would have let Colby go if he, Jase, hadn't been there to intervene. In Jase's estimation Steven Duncan was a man to command absolute and unfailing obedience from his subordinates, and Davis had been his personal secretary for ten years. His habit of obedience

36

must be well developed, yet he had backed away from the advancing Colby as from a rabid vixen.

Maybe she had a lover she was desperate to return to. His face hardened. Mrs. Butler would have his hide if he foisted some cheap little tramp off on her, especially since Paul was just now starting to come of age. A thirteen-year-old boy who's recently lost his parents was very vulnerable. A bored, resentful little tart could really stir up a hornets' nest, just for amusement's sake.

Well, he'd just have to lay it on the line for her. She was to stay away from Paul, and if she gave Mrs. Butler any trouble, he'd tan that sexy little rear of hers black and blue. He might owe Steven Duncan a favor for the help he'd given Jase's father long ago, but that didn't include wrecking Mrs. Butler's life or that of her orphaned grandson. She was a friend as well as his housekeeper and he'd see that no more tragedy came to her life. The loss of her only daughter had been a blow she was still reeling from. He wouldn't allow Colby Duncan to be a last straw!

That grim resolve tautened the planes of his face and his hands tightened on the control yoke. He must have been mad to have agreed to this scheme, but Steven Duncan had consummately played the desperately concerned father, and before he knew it, Jase had discovered that he had promised to aid and abet him in the kidnapping of his daughter.

The debt of the father had descended on the son and it was a powerful debt. Steven Duncan had come to the rescue long ago when Brad Culhane's business was foundering and had pulled it around at some considerable personal sacrifice to himself. His father had confessed that he had been contemplating suicide at the time and Steven Duncan had literally given him a new lease on life. Culhanes always paid their debts, so when Steven Duncan asked Jase's help in getting his daughter away from unsavory associations, there wasn't much to do but say yes. Jase just hoped he wasn't going to regret it any more than he already did.

They began the descent into a small airfield in silence. Colby had given up in her attempt to elicit information from a taciturn Jase and, half turned away from him, the limit her seat belt would allow, dozed uneasily in the seat. She woke as the plane began to bank and then straightened out, but in a nose-down attitude. As they lost altitude she saw the lights of a small airfield beneath them, and in the distance, a small town's lights winked in ordered regularity.

"Refueling stop," Jase informed her succinctly. He concentrated on the landing pattern, and Colby felt the bump as the landing gear extended. It was a smooth touchdown, even though the only field illumination was that of the landing lights that picked out the length of the runway.

Jase taxied the plane over to the small cluster of buildings and turned off the engines. As Colby began to unbuckle her seat belt he said, "And where do you think you're going, Miss Duncan? I told you this is only a refueling stop. We'll be taking off again in a few minutes."

Colby continued divesting herself of the hindering buckles and got up out of the seat. "I'm going to stretch my legs and I presume there is a bathroom somewhere nearby." She looked him straight in the eye. "I don't even know what state we're in, let alone what town. Just where do you expect me to go? The town I saw from the air looked several miles away. Are you afraid you can't run me down if I take off for it?"

She looked scornfully down at herself. "I'm really not

38

dressed for a five- or ten-mile hike, and this airport is hardly bustling with taxi service, is it?"

"Hardly," he admitted dryly. There was only one attendant on duty and he was there because Jase had arranged in advance for him to be on hand for the refueling. He supposed it wouldn't hurt to let her walk around a bit, and he'd make sure she kept away from the one man on duty.

"All right," he agreed. "But you'll keep away from the attendant. I want your word on that or you'll be locked here in the plane."

"What, you mean you're willing to take my word on something?" Colby feigned stunned amazement.

Jase didn't smile. "I'm capable of enforcing it, Miss Duncan. Dressed as you are, your credibility isn't very high. Don't put me to the trouble of having to make up a story to explain any wild accusations you might feel compelled to make. I assure you, my word will be taken before yours, and whatever story I might have to concoct will surely not redound to your credit."

Colby said tightly, "The position is clear. I'll have no contact with the attendant. And now, if you don't mind, I'd really like to find a bathroom."

Jase nodded curtly and preceded her down the aisle. He opened the hatch and extended the steps, descending before her and holding out a hand to help her down. She looked down at the outstretched hand, up to his face, and her lip curled. She came agilely down the steps in spite of her tight dress and high-heeled shoes, ignoring pointedly the proffered helping hand.

Jase felt the heat run up the back of his neck. Lord, she was a provoking little madam!

Colby headed directly for the building she assumed would house the bathroom and whatever waiting-room facilities this small airfield boasted. She intended to wash her face, but her primary aim was to find a pay phone. She didn't expect Jase would think to guard against that, and she had to get a call through to Matt. If she couldn't get away from Jase through her own efforts, then she'd have to depend on Matt to spring her somehow. And he must be frantic by now, because he'd know that she wouldn't voluntarily miss being at the club. Her father wouldn't admit to kidnapping his own daughter, and all Matt would get from him would be bland denials of any knowledge of her whereabouts.

Colby's steps faltered momentarily. Come to think of it, kidnapping was a rather drastic way of registering disapproval of her singing career. She considered the implications of that startling thought. So much had happened in so short a time that she really hadn't stopped to think why her father had had her kidnapped. The simple fact that he *had* had so consumed her with rage that she had only been concerned with getting away.

Could he know of her involvement with the police? Her father was a very astute man. Had her "rebellion" rung so false to him that in searching for a reason for her insistence on staying at the club he had somehow divined the true motivation? He had known of her bitter rage at the waste of Sandi's tragic death, known too that Sandi had frequented the club. Many of their crowd did. He was more than capable of putting fractions together and coming up with a whole number.

Well, whether he knew or not, the end result was the same, and she was still left with the problem of escape. Once she was away, the other could be sorted out, and she'd see that further interference became impossible. A threat of prosecution against Davis and what's-his-name would bind her father's hands most effectively, and it would be no idle bluff. She was still seething.

Jase opened the door for Colby and followed her into the building. It was little more than a box, with two doors appropriately marked and labeled with the international pictographs for male and female and an uncomfortable-looking couch flanked by end tables bearing vintage *National Geographic*s. Colby saw a pay phone attached to the wall, but not a flicker of the relief she felt crossed her face. She went directly toward the door marked LADIES and closed it firmly behind her.

Jase watched her cross the room, looking neither to the left or the right. That dress must have been sprayed on! There was a lovely, proud sweep to her spine, and her walk had a gliding grace that would have put a cat to shame. He shook his head at his fancies. So young to have started on such a disastrously wrong road. Too much money and not enough spankings, he supposed.

He checked the bare room. There were no windows big enough for her to climb out of in the bathroom, and the only ones in the waiting room would be in sight as he supervised the refueling operation. He went back out to the plane, convinced there was no mischief she could get up to for the moment.

Colby scrubbed her face, sighing as the annoying make-up rinsed down the drain. The liquid soap dried her skin, but the natural oils would soothe that tight, stretched feeling soon. It was worth it to have her normal face back.

She listened cautiously at the door but could hear nothing. She opened the door gently and swept the room with a comprehensive glance. Empty. He was somewhere outside, probably watching the refueling. She'd only have a few minutes, she was sure. She pulled coins from her purse and darted over to the phone, dialing frantically. She gave the operator her credit card number and Matt's home phone number.

The phone rang only once and was answered almost before it had completed even that. "MacGuire!" was snapped into the phone. He must have been right by it, Colby realized.

"Matt, it's Colby. Just listen, I've probably only got moments." She rushed on. "I've been kidnapped, but my father's behind it, not our friends from the club. I've been flown off in a private plane, a twin-engine job, and I don't know where I am. The pilot is some cowboy type, first name Jase—"

The receiver was snatched from her hand and slammed back into its rest. Hard hands grasped her shoulders and swung her around, shaking her violently as they turned her. Her purse dropped at her feet and her head jolted on her shoulders.

Jase had been standing out by the plane and had looked idly toward the windows. He saw Colby reenter the room and cross swiftly out of his line of vision. The very purposefulness of her movements triggered an alarm and he went toward the building. By the time he got there, she had completed her call, and when he opened the door, he paused for a moment, listening.

He heard the whole of the breathless, hurried words and was furious with himself for giving her a chance to say even that much. He didn't know who Matt was, probably her boyfriend, and he didn't know what this Matt could do about the situation, but the fewer people who knew about this whole thing the better. Since Colby was still underage, her father technically had grounds, but still. . . .

Even as these thoughts flashed through his mind, Jase was shaking Colby. He was furious with her and with himself for giving her the opportunity to make more trouble so he shook her until her teeth rattled.

Colby tried to get her breath as Jase manhandled her, and when he stopped shaking her and released her shoulders, she gulped in air and clenched her right hand into a fist. There was a red mist before her eyes, and the Irish side of her heritage blazed out of control. She swung on him.

It was no ladylike tap she tried. She let go with a closed fist, roundhouse right that could have dislocated his jaw if it had happened to have landed. He felt the shock of it in his blocking arm, which he barely got up in time. When he blocked her punch, Colby kicked him as hard as she could in the shin. Jase yelled and leaped back, out of range.

He didn't have time to rub his aching leg because Colby, adrenaline pumping freely through her racing bloodstream, carried the fight to him. All the fury she had been nursing since she realized what was happening had boiled over and she was literally fighting-mad.

Jase had a hard time fending off the swirling fury who leaped at him. He didn't want to hurt her, but no such considerations governed Colby, so it was a breathless few minutes before he managed to imprison her facedown across his lap. He began to spank her with gusto.

Colby yelled and bit him hard on the thigh.

"Dammit to hell!" Jase let her go abruptly and she scrambled swiftly away from him. She snatched up one of her high-heeled shoes, both of which had fallen off, and backed up against a wall, ready to throw it at him or use it if he came toward her again.

"You meant that," he accused her wonderingly as he rubbed his thigh. He would bear the teeth marks for several days, which would have occasioned considerable comment had anyone seen them before they faded!

"You're damn right I did," Colby snarled at him. "You may have kidnapped me, but it gives you no license to manhandle me!"

Jase didn't answer her right away. He was staring at her strangely. Colby stared right back, alert for any sudden move. Jase couldn't believe his eyes. Gone was the hard, artificial, older-than-her-years woman. Facing him instead was a stunningly lovely young girl, hair disheveled and eyes almost black with unsuppressed rage, but she was gorgeous. Her skin had the smooth freshness of healthy youth and her mouth was enchantingly shaped, even though the lower lip was pulled taut with anger. He hadn't noticed the classic perfection of her nose before, and the pinched whiteness about the nostrils detracted not an iota from its short, patrician line.

Her eyelashes were still the same. Could they possibly be real? His eyes dropped down the length of her body, noting in passing the deep breaths she drew that made her breasts surge tautly against the low-cut neck of her dress. The dress was the same, and the body within it, but somehow the face and the body now affected him strangely, where before he had been able to dismiss them with contempt.

"Who is Matt?" he rasped.

"None of your business," she shot back smartly.

"Is he your lover?" Jase pressed her.

"And if he is?" Colby taunted him.

Jase's face darkened and he took a half step toward her. Colby raised the shoe she held, heel outward. Jase stopped. Colby eyed him with baleful animosity and stayed alert.

Jase rested his hands on his hips and spoke in firm tones. "You, Miss Colby Duncan, are a rich little bitch, too pretty for your own good, and too spoiled for the good of others. Now, we are going to go back out to that plane and we are going to get in it and complete our journey. You will walk out on your own two feet or I will carry you out. Put down that shoe; put it and the other one back on those deadly little feet of yours and head them out the door. I'll be right behind you, and I won't touch you if you behave yourself. You have my word. You also have my promise that if you give me any more trouble I will make you extremely sorry and unable to sit down for a week."

Colby could have told him that she was already going to be unable to sit comfortably for a while. Those sharp swats he had got in before she bit him had left her longing to rub her posterior. Pride forbade it, but a pillow would not have come amiss as a welcome addition to the seat cushion of the plane's copilot's chair. The imprint of that hard palm and long fingers would be with her for a while, as her teethmarks would be with him.

Someone was going to pay for the indignities she had suffered this night, pay full measure, pressed down and running over. The last time she'd been spanked she had been four years old and had deserved every bit of it. But she was not a four-year-old now!

She balanced herself on one foot and bent over to put on the shoe she had been holding in her hand. Jase bent down and picked up her other shoe, which had been lying near his foot. He held it out to her and she took it gingerly from him, moving back and away as soon as she had it in her hand. Jase tilted a sardonic eyebrow at her and she looked at him expressionlessly.

She slipped on the other shoe and walked over to her purse near the phone, where it had been kicked in the struggle. If she looked ruefully at the phone, Jase didn't see it, for her back was to him. She picked up the purse and checked the clasp to be sure it hadn't loosened when it hit the ground.

Then she walked past the waiting man and out the door, heading directly toward the plane. She was in the plane before Jase had covered half the distance to it. She wished she knew how to fly. She'd love to have been able to lock him out and take off, leaving him shaking an impotent fist at the sky and her, a dwindling speck. Maybe she'd take lessons when this was all over. She grinned mockingly to herself. *You never know . . . I might be kidnapped again someday!*

Jase was in no happy frame of mind himself. It had seemed relatively simple to him when Steven had told him what was planned. He'd fly in, wait for Davis and—What was his name? Oh, yes, Motham—to bring the girl to the airport. They'd get in the plane and he'd bring her to the ranch. Steven had said she'd probably sulk a bit, but not that she'd do her best to take a chunk out of his hide or dislocate his jaw. He was a man who had expected to pick up a sulky kitten and had instead come up holding a spitting, clawing wildcat.

By the time he got into the cockpit, Colby was already strapped in again and was looking determinedly out the window. He didn't know it, but she had spent those few moments of privacy briskly rubbing her posterior in an effort to ease the stinging discomfort. It hadn't helped much and she wished she could ease the uncomfortable pressure by tucking her feet up under herself and rolling her hips over to sit on the side of her buttocks. It really hurt to sit down flat! Damn Jase anyway. He needn't have spanked her so hard, she thought resentfully, completely forgetting that she had sunk her teeth into his leg with intent to do bodily injury.

Anyway, her dress was too tight to tuck her legs up beneath her unless she exposed considerably more leg than she had a mind to in front of him. How she wished for a pair of comfortable jeans. They must have packed at least a pair or two.

Jase took his place and, with a brief wave to the watching attendant, taxied the plane and took off. Colby stared out of the window, turning the line of her determined little chin and long, slender neck in profile to him. A small muscle was knotted at the angle of her jaw. Jase thought it was anger. Colby knew it came from her discomfort.

They flew on in silence. Jase shot occasional glances at Colby but she continued to stare out of the window. His shin throbbed, there was an ache in his thigh, and he had a few sore spots on his ribs where her elbows and flailing fists had connected. He felt almost as though he'd come out on the losing end of a barroom brawl. This abduction was certainly not running smoothly!

Colby was tired. She would have loved to try to sleep but the area Jase had so forcefully paddled protested too much. So, she looked out the window. It gave her an excuse to lean to one side and thus relieve the pressure. They flew on and on over generally unrelieved blackness. Occasionally she would see a small, scattered cluster of lights to the left or the right of them, and once, far to the right, the larger sprawl of a medium-size town, but otherwise they were alone, a small island of life in the darkness.

47

Cast away with a man I can't stand, she thought humorously. *The man I'd least like to be marooned with! Oh, well, there'll be other people at the ranch,* she consoled herself. *Surely he'll be out "riding the ranges" or mending the fences most of the time. He said there was a young boy I'm not to be a bad influence upon, so there must be a wife on the premises. I wonder how old his boy is. Probably not much more than a toddler. He doesn't look old enough to have children who are much grown, and he doesn't look like a man who married very early.*

I wonder just what his wife is going to think about having an unwilling guest foisted upon her. I wonder if he told her he was going to kidnap *his unwilling guest.* Colby's mouth twitched. *Well, if he hasn't told her, I sure will, loud and clear!*

Another small cluster of lights was coming up, dead ahead. It seemed as though they had been flying for days. Colby didn't try to smother the large yawn that stretched her mouth. Presumably he was going to give her a bed to sleep on at the ranch, and right now she wouldn't care if it was stuffed with cornhusks, just as long as it was flat and had a sheet to curl up under. She'd even skip the sheet; to lie flat on her stomach was going to be heaven enough.

They were heading toward that cluster of lights. She hoped it was the ranch and not another refueling stop. Maybe this was really some sequential nightmare and they'd just fly on and on forever, down for refueling and back into the air again.

No, it had to be a private field. There was a hangar and a Jeep parked beside it, but not much else. The place was deserted. Jase taxied the plane to a stop near the hangar. "We're here," he announced briefly and stretched his arms and shoulders wearily.

Colby released herself from the seat, but didn't get up right away. She looked up at Jase as he loomed over her, her eyes shielded by those ridiculously long eyelashes. She noticed the signs of weariness, the tired lines of his face as he looked inscrutably down at her. If he'd made this flight twice today, to and from, no wonder he was tired. His hand was unconsciously massaging his thigh where she'd bitten him and she smiled with enjoyment. Jase noticed the direction of her gaze and correctly interpreted the cause of her smile. His mouth tightened to a thin line.

"Get up," he ordered her shortly. "This is the end of the line and I don't propose to carry all your luggage by myself."

"You mean there's no skycap service at your airport?" she mocked waspishly. "How too, too fatiguing and provincial! What if I refuse? I thought I was an honored guest at your charming establishment, Jase."

"Get up, Colby!" he thundered. "So help me, girl, if you give me any more lip, I won't be responsible for my actions. We're going to get a few things straight, but before we do, I want you off this plane and carrying bags over to that Jeep. Now move."

Colby prudently got up, but her progress down the aisle was a languid stroll, not a terrified scuttle, or at least as languid a stroll as one can manage when one has to walk slightly stooped to avoid the low roof of the plane. Jase watched her with unwilling admiration. She never gave an inch. If he'd roared at one of his cowboys that way, that man would have hit the ground running.

Colby waited for him to undo the hatch, ostentatiously leaning back out of his way to avoid coming into contact with any part of his body. Jase's eyes went a peculiar silvery color and she felt a momentary qualm that she hoped didn't show on her face. Just for a moment he had looked as though he was torn between killing or kissing her, and she didn't want to provoke him into doing either, she thought shakily.

She had read Jase's mind exactly. He'd never met a woman before who could make him lose his temper so readily. He'd never laid violent hands on a woman in his life, but if he wasn't careful, he was going to end up either strangling or raping this one. From the moment he had laid eyes on her, he had been roiled by powerful emotions and he didn't like it one bit. Damn Steven Duncan and his brat of a daughter!

He opened the hatch and deployed the ladder, then turned and deliberately brushed past Colby as he went to the rear to the luggage compartment where her bags had been put. They must have packed every stitch of clothing she owned, and he could only hope that there was something suitable in one of those cases for ranch wear. He certainly wouldn't allow her to parade around in getups like she was wearing right now. He'd never get a lick of work out of any of his men.

As Jase began to pull out bag after bag, Colby was unconsciously echoing his thoughts. They must have cleaned out all her closets and drawers. It looked as though her father were sending her for a protracted exile. On the bright side, if they'd packed everything, at least her jeans and shirts would have been included. From the weight of the bags Jase handed her, they'd put all her shoes in as well. This one must have her hiking boots in it.

Jase preceded her down the steps, as he had before, and Colby silently hefted the bags down to him, one at a time. When they were all unloaded, Jase stood by the steps, waiting for Colby herself to descend. This time he didn't hold out a helping hand. He'd catch her if she started to fall, but he wouldn't risk another rebuff of his automatic courtesy.

As before, Colby negotiated the steps without difficulty and didn't outwardly register by so much as a flicker the effort it cost her. She was tired and stiff from sitting so long but she'd have crawled down on her hands and knees before she accepted a hand from Jase.

When she was safely down, he buttoned the hatch back up and indicated the two smaller bags with the toe of his boot. "Yours."

Colby obediently picked them up and headed toward the Jeep. Jase followed with the three larger bags, leading Colby to muse silently, *Good grief, he's strong,* for he carried the heavy, ungainly load with absolutely no sign of strain.

He piled the luggage into the back of the Jeep, left her standing while he turned off the airfield lights, and then climbed in the driver's seat. Colby hadn't gotten in yet and he shot her a sardonic look she couldn't see in the dark. "Prefer to walk? It's two miles to the house and the track is pretty rough."

She climbed into her seat with alacrity. He'd probably leave her if she didn't, she acknowledged. He knew she couldn't go anywhere out here in the middle of Lord-knows-where, and if he didn't leave her, he'd probably pick her up and drop her into the seat with no tender care. She preferred to climb in under her own power and with some semblance of dignity.

When she was seated beside him, Jase didn't start the engine right away, as she had expected. It was nearly three A.M. by her watch, though who knew what time zone she

51

was in now, and she had expected him to be eager to get home. He sat, staring out through the windshield, forearms draped over the steering wheel. Since it was starlight dark outside, and he hadn't turned on the Jeep's headlights he couldn't be looking at anything. . . .

Colby yawned several times, uncontrollably, and shifted restlessly in her hard seat. Why didn't he get going? She for one didn't fancy spending the rest of what remained of the night sitting uncomfortably upright in a Jeep seat. She was just preparing to tell him so when he moved abruptly.

Jase half turned so that he could look directly at her. Her face glimmered in the starlight, floating with disembodied paleness in the dark aura of her cloudy black hair. "Before we go up to the main ranch, we're going to get something straight, Colby," he informed her.

At least he's dropped the "Miss" Duncan, Colby realized. *I guess you can't continue to be on such formal terms with a woman whose teeth marks are sunk in your leg.* She listened to him attentively.

"You will behave yourself while you're under my roof, Colby. Mrs. Butler, my housekeeper, has had a hard time recently and I won't have you adding to her burdens. Her daughter and son-in-law were killed in a car accident six months ago, and their son, her only grandchild, was injured too. He's living with her now and is recuperating well, slowly regaining his strength and mental balance. He's turned thirteen. I don't want his total recovery set back in any way. Do you understand what I'm saying to you?"

"No," Colby answered him. If he had a housekeeper, what did his wife do all day? "What have I got to do with his recovery, or lack of it?"

"I don't want you flirting with him out of boredom or for sheer spite," Jase said bluntly. "He's at a very vulnerable age, just coming into manhood, and you could do him a lot of damage if you play your big-city games with him because you haven't anything better to do. You're pretty when you have that gunk off your face, and he's old enough to respond to that."

If he could have seen the rapidly shifting expressions on Colby's face after that remarkable statement, he would have been a worried man. Her first reaction was sheer, stunned amazement. What in the world would she be doing flirting with a thirteen-year-old child, for heaven's sake? A baby eight years younger than herself! Her second reaction was outrage that he would accuse her of even considering such a despicable trick, of being capable of such revolting behavior out of nothing more than boredom. How dare he! Just what kind of person did he think she was? What a low and nasty mind the man must have.

When she finally found her voice, it shook slightly, but was even enough. "I think you're warning me off, is that the correct term? I'm not to use my feminine wiles on your housekeeper's grandson. Does that mean you're prepared to offer me alternative targets if my desire for masculine companionship gets the better of me? I mean, after all, if I need a man so badly that I'll settle for a thirteen-year-old boy, then certainly you must be prepared to offer a substitute. Got any eighty-year-old grandfathers I can fascinate?" By now she was shaking all over with suppressed rage, and her voice was little more than a hissing whisper.

He started to speak, but she continued, "Listen to me, Jase Whoever-you-are. I have had enough. I have been kidnapped, manhandled, and now insulted in the most degrading fashion possible. If you don't start up this Jeep right now, I am going to get out and start walking and I don't particularly care where I end up. Any place would be better than sitting here next to a man I loathe and having to listen to him malign my character and my morals. I have nothing more to say to you and I hope to God you have nothing more to say to me."

Jase started the Jeep's engine and gunned it. Colby grabbed the seat and held on for dear life as they jounced and jolted over the track. He must have made the distance to the main house in record time. Although he slowed as they approached the house, she didn't for a moment think it was out of consideration for her bones. He probably didn't want to rouse the household. After all, thirteen-year-old boys need their sleep if they're going to have the strength to withstand the wiles of a latter-day Delilah, she seethed.

It was too dark to make out much about the house except it was big, two storied, and had a wide front porch, overhung by a sloping roof. Jase got out of the Jeep and carried two of the larger suitcases up to the porch. Colby got out the ones she had been responsible for previously and took them up as well. Jase opened the front door and flicked a switch on just inside. The entrance hall was flooded with light, which spilled out onto the front porch.

Colby squinted as the light assaulted her eyeballs. She followed Jase to a set of graceful stairs curving up from the hall, her steps wearily dragging. She had started to carry the suitcases with her, and the stairs had loomed as high as the Alps, but Jase said curtly, "Leave them. I'll bring them all up after I've shown you your room."

Thankfully she obeyed and trailed him, several steps lower. He seemed to be making no effort to go quietly and Colby thought that his wife must be the soundest sleeper ever born. Even a deaf man could have heard Jase's boots clumping down the hall, carpeted floors or not. He stopped in front of a closed door and set down one of the two suitcases he was carrying to free his right hand. He opened the door, flicked another switch, and went into the room after picking up the suitcase he had momentarily set down.

Colby followed him to the door and stood looking into the room. It was a large room, with airy, high ceilings and two windows set into the wall across the room. A wall-to-wall closet ran the width of a second wall, with alternating panels of full-length mirrored surfaces. A large double bed dominated the third wall with a headboard, bookcase, and built-in nightstands forming part of the whole unit. There were several dressers and tall drawer chests, a comfortable-looking recliner chair, and low table, complete with a good reading lamp. It was a well-planned room and had an impersonal, untenanted air, in spite of the small low bowl of flowers on one of the nightstands by the bed. Most definitely a guest room, Colby concluded, but she would be comfortable, for as long as she had to stay. Heaven send it wouldn't be long!

Jase put the two bags down on the floor and said, "I'll go get the other bags. The bathroom is this way." She followed him out and he pointed to a door some two doors away. "Take a shower if you want to," he offered.

"But it'll wake everyone up," she protested instinctively, and foolishly, she realized a moment after the words left her mouth. If anyone had been going to wake up, they certainly would have done so by now!

"Mrs. Butler and Paul have their own self-contained unit in a small house out back. You won't disturb them," he assured her.

"But your wife . . . your children. . . ." Colby let the words trail away.

"It would be hard to wake them," Jase said, grinning mockingly, "since they don't exist as yet. I'm not married, Miss Duncan."

"Oh."

"Yes, oh." His grin was sardonic. "You're alone in the house with me, but since you're no shrinking violet, that shouldn't worry you overmuch."

He wheeled abruptly and headed back toward the stairs. "It doesn't bother me in the least, Jase," she said to his retreating back as nastily as she could. "I'm sure I have nothing to fear from *you!*"

He stopped abruptly and spun around. Colby was walking toward the bathroom, a derisively provocative sway to her hips. Jase watched her go in and shut the door, his fists clenching and unclenching, his face a grim mask.

As soon as Colby heard him thunder down the stairs, she whipped back into the bedroom he had assigned her and threw one of the cases upon the bed. She rummaged through it swiftly. Nothing useful. She craved a shower, tired as she was, but she didn't own much in the way of nightwear, because generally she slept nude. She listened anxiously for sounds of Jase's return, but heard nothing. She didn't want another run-in with him tonight.

The second suitcase yielded a knit nightshirt a friend had given her as a joke gift on her twenty-first birthday. It had PRIME RIB emblazoned across the chest in big purple letters, but at least it covered her past midthigh. She also unearthed her makeup kit and toothbrush, so she headed toward the bathroom with cleansing cream, toothbrush, and sleepwear clutched in her hands. She'd have to purloin some toothpaste from the bathroom, since hers either hadn't been included or had been put in another suitcase. Jase might be bringing the rest of her suitcases up at any minute and she planned to be locked safely behind the bathroom door when he did. No man likes to have it implied that he is impotent and incapable, and she didn't want to see him again until they were in the presence of other people.

She took a swift hot-as-she-could-stand-it shower, cleansed her face, and brushed her teeth. She felt almost human again, except that there seemed to be sand somewhere behind her eyeballs and beneath her eyelids. She yawned again and tidied up the bathroom, folding the used towels and washcloth neatly over the drying rack. The bed hadn't bounced like it was corncob-stuffed when she'd dropped her suitcases on it and she was longing to test it for herself . . . for about an eight-to-ten-hour test, she thought.

She gathered her dress, briefs, nylons, and shoes in a bundle. (The dress hadn't allowed for a bra.) She didn't think she'd ever feel comfortable in that dress again—not that she had felt comfortable in the dress before, but it had been a good working dress. She peeked cautiously out of the door but heard nothing. Light spilled from her door, but the rest of the hall was dark again. There was a thin line of light beneath a door farther on down the hall, presumably from Jase's room.

With commendable speed she zipped down the hall and into her room and shut the door behind her with a gasp of relief. The gasp turned to a gulp of horror when she looked over at the bed, and she clutched the clothes and shoes to her with defensive instinct.

Jase watched the color run up into her cheeks and her violet-blue eyes widen until they seemed to fill her face.

Her silky black hair tumbled in disorder around her face and shoulders, little tendrils curling wispily from the steam moisture of her recent shower. For the first time he could believe she was seventeen, with her bare toes curling and uncurling in the pile of the carpet.

Colby simply gazed in stupefaction at Jase as he lounged at ease on the bed, his silver-gray eyes hooded by the shadows over his face. *Me and my big mouth,* she thought miserably. *I just couldn't resist one last insult. Colby, you cretinous dolt, you've really dumped yourself in hot water this time.*

She stood by the door. If he took one step toward her, she'd be out the door and down the stairs before he could take a second. She wasn't hindered by a tight dress and high-heeled shoes now, and even if she didn't know the terrain, she'd take her chances with the great outdoors before she'd chance the great indoors with Jase.

When she showed no signs of either speaking or moving away from the safety of the door, Jase grinned in actual enjoyment. The expression on her face when she'd come into the room had been priceless. He rubbed his thigh meditatively and watched her eyes narrow warily.

"We didn't finish our talk in the Jeep, Colby," he informed her smoothly. "There are a few more points I want to make clear."

Her expression grew rigidly blank and her eyes went dark blue and stormy. "I think you managed to cover everything in insulting detail, Jase. I don't want to hear any more strictures on moral behavior from you."

He hesitated and she could almost believe for a moment he looked uncomfortable and a bit regretful, but the shadows on his face were deceptive and she thought she'd probably imagined it. Certainly what he said next in no way constituted an apology. He was giving her orders again!

"What I have to say concerns Mrs. Butler. First of all, she doesn't know why you're here. As far as she's concerned, you're the daughter of a friend of mine, come to experience ranch life firsthand and to enjoy a quiet vacation. You won't tell her any differently." He gave her a hard look. She gave him an equally hard one back and said nothing. "The second thing is," he continued, "that you won't cause her any unnecessary work. That means no trays for breakfast in bed and you'll take care of your own room. She doesn't have time to pick up after you and make your bed. I don't imagine you're much use around a house, so just try not to get in her way. This is a big house and she has all she can do to keep up with it and see to Paul's lessons. He's doing correspondence courses until he's ready to go back to school."

He stood up, looking gigantic, and the shadow he threw stretched menacingly wide. "Forget your big-city values while you're here and you'll come to no harm. I have a fairly well-stocked library and a good stereo set. I'll show you how to work it in a day or so. We have a lot of magazines and there's always a jigsaw puzzle set up in the library if you really get desperate. When I get time, I might even teach you how to ride."

Something changed in her face slightly, a muscle flicker, no more. He looked at her sharply. "You're not afraid of horses, are you?"

"No, Jase, I'm not afraid of horses," she assured him.

"I've brought up all your luggage." He gestured to three other suitcases piled by the closet. "If you need anything else that wasn't packed, you can ask Mrs. Butler for it in the morning." He walked toward the door and she moved away from it, giving him wide berth.

He opened the door and looked her up and down thoroughly. "Good night, Colby. Pleasant dreams."

The look she gave him assured that if they were pleasant they wouldn't contain him anywhere. He chuckled and went out, closing the door softly behind him. She darted over to it and turned the key loudly in the lock, withdrawing it afterward and tossing it on the nearest nightstand. She heard him laughing all the way down the hall.

Colby threw the bundle of clothes she had been clutching against her chest to the floor with some violence. She stalked over to the bed, yanked back the spread, blankets, and sheet, and ferociously plumped the pillow Jase had been leaning against. She wanted no imprint of him in her bed.

Only the bedside lamp remained on in the room. Jase must have turned out the overhead one when he brought her suitcases up. She slid into bed and wriggled sensuously against the smooth, clean, cool sheets. Ah, bliss. A too-enthusiastic wiggle reminded her of her tender rump and she flipped over onto her stomach with a muttered malediction spared for Jase. The nightshirt promptly crept up around her waist, twisting into an uncomfortable lump at the same time.

She sat back up with a stronger oath, stripped it off over her head, and dropped it by the side of the bed. She'd put it on if there was a fire, but if she tried to sleep in it, it would probably creep up around her neck and save Jase the trouble of strangling her.

She switched off the light and snuggled back down into the pillow, facedown. She was asleep in ten seconds.

She didn't hear the key turn in the lock when she didn't

answer the soft tap. When the door opened quietly, a rumpled black head peered around the edge of the door. Silvery eyes widened slightly at the sight of her as she lay, facedown on the bed. The sheet had worked its way down to her waist and one arm dangled half off the edge of the bed. The nightshirt lay crumpled by the bed. Her body was turned away from the door and her mass of dark hair spilled onto the white sheet in a dusky flood.

He had only meant to assure himself that she was still in the room. He wouldn't have put it past her to have gone out of the window and started a cross-country hike. She had guts, he had to give her that! She also had a beautiful back. He restrained his wandering imagination firmly and shut the door as gently as he opened it. The key clicked softly in the lock. Colby slept on.

She woke an hour later and stretched sinuously. There was no disorientation, no "Where am I?" question in her mind. She remembered it all, every horrible, painful bit of it. She groaned softly and reached a hand back to feel her buttocks, kneading gently to determine the extent of residual bruising. Hmmm, not too bad. An occasional tender spot, but on the whole, not bad.

Sunlight shone strongly into the room and there were sounds of various activities outside. A rancher's work was never done and she devoutly hoped Jase was well into his daily activities. She needed a cup of coffee badly, and she would much rather meet Mrs. Butler without his piercing gray eyes watching her every move.

She slid out of bed and made it deftly, with no wasted motion. Not handy around the house, indeed. She snorted inelegantly. The first suitcase she had opened last night had contained her favorite jeans and shirt plus a jumble of clean underwear. She would bet some man had packed up her clothes, she thought with stormy blue eyes. No woman would have treated fine lingerie so disrespectfully. It was her one clothes extravagance. She loved sexy, silky underwear, and her bras and briefs were generally mere wisps of lace and silk. She pulled on a paired set of ecru bra and briefs that nearly matched her skin color.

The jeans were serviceable blue denim, softly faded from many washings and they curved to her figure in a way Levi Strauss would never have believed possible. Her shirt was of the same denim, equally softly faded, with patch pockets and short sleeves. She found a pair of heavy white crew socks and pulled them on, then lifted on to the bed the suitcase she suspected of harboring her sneakers. It did hold her sneakers, plus a pair of hiking boots, as well as other assorted shoes, all tossed in together. Definitely a man! A woman would have at least wrapped the shoes in pairs, not just dumped them all in together. Damn, damn, damn! The thought of some man pawing through her personal belongings was galling. She'd chew her father's ears down to bare nubs when she saw him next.

She ran a hasty brush through her hair and tied it into two low ponytails behind her ears, securing them with some rubber bands she found in her purse. The hairstyle made her look about ten years old, but it kept her hair back from her face.

She made a quick foray to the bathroom, brushed her teeth, and splashed icy cold water on her face. She desperately needed a cup of coffee. She cat-footed to the top of the stairs and listened intently. She couldn't hear a thing. Well, there was nothing for it. She would have to go down sometime. Hanging around wouldn't get her that much-needed cup of coffee, and if her stomach wasn't lying to her, it was lunch and breakfast time all rolled up into one.

CHAPTER THREE

Colby went downstairs and turned toward the back of the house. Instinct told her that the kitchen would be in that direction, and her nose soon informed her that her instinct had the right idea. Someone, presumably Mrs. Butler, was baking bread. It was one of Colby's favorite hobbies and she had some special recipes she had developed on her own. Maybe Mrs. Butler would like— She pulled her idle thoughts to a jerking halt. She wouldn't be here long enough to exchange recipes with Mrs. Butler.

She went boldly down the hall and pushed open a swinging door. A spare gray-haired woman with kind brown eyes looked up from the mound of dough she was kneading. She immediately left the dough and walked over to the sink to wash her flour-dusted hands. "Come in, my dear, come in," she said over her shoulder. "I'm Mrs. Butler, Jase's housekeeper, and you must be Colby. You must also be starving. Jase said you hadn't got in until after four this morning. Would you like some coffee to be going on with until I can rustle you up a snack?"

"A cup of coffee would be wonderful, Mrs. Butler. Thank you very much," Colby answered as she advanced further into the room. She lifted her head and sniffed appreciatively, and Mrs. Butler laughed.

"There's some just out of the oven cool enough to cut. With butter and jelly or just butter?"

"Just butter," Colby laughed. "Anything else on freshly baked bread is little short of sacrilege. Which loaf shall I cut? May I have the heel?" she asked diffidently.

"Of course, my dear. The first loaf cut never lasts long enough to dry out anyway," she spoke out of long experience as a breadmaker.

"I know," Colby agreed readily. "When I'm making it, I've been known to go through a whole loaf all by myself, hot from the oven. And that's a greedy admission since I live alone. I even"—her voice dropped conspiratorially—"use full-size loaf pans. It's an addiction. One slice and the whole loaf is doomed."

Mrs. Butler chuckled and handed her a serrated-edge bread knife, pointing to a golden-brown loaf cooling on a rack. She poured a cup of coffee for Colby, pushed sugar and the milk jug along the counter, and laid a knife on the butter dish, ready for use after Colby had made her incision into the sacrificial loaf.

Colby wolfed down the butter-dripping heel with delicate greed and slowed slightly as she bit into the second slice. Mrs. Butler watched her indulgently as she finished that slice as well. Colby sighed happily and licked a few driblets of butter from her fingers.

"If you butter a cat's paws, it'll stay at its new home," a sardonic voice drawled from the doorway.

Colby whirled to find Jase watching her from the doorway she had so recently come through herself. He inspected her clothes, secretly surprised that they displayed such evidence of well-worn comfort. Colby showed no immediate desire to greet him civilly so he continued: "I looked in on you upstairs, but found you gone. I see you've met

Mrs. Butler. Margy, may I have some of that bread too?" He managed somehow to look like a mischievous little boy.

"See, Colby," Mrs. Butler chuckled, "just what I said. The first loaf doesn't ever have a chance to get cold. Of course, Jase, help yourself and while you're at it, cut me a slice too. No reason for the cook to pass up the fruits of her labors."

Jase held out his hand for the bread knife that Colby had been holding as she prepared to cut another slice. She looked at him for a long moment and then reversed it, handing it to him handle first. Their fingers touched and she felt his, warm and hard, against hers for a fleeting instant before she withdrew her own, leaving him in possession of the knife.

Jase began to slice into the loaf, cutting two pieces with neat dispatch. "Would you like another piece, Colby?" he asked her politely, waiting with the knife poised.

Colby's look assured him silently, *Not if I were starving to death,* but she said aloud with chill politeness, "No, thank you."

Mrs. Butler observed this byplay with some surprise, especially since Colby had obviously been going to cut herself another slice before Jase came into the room. Jase's eyes narrowed warningly, a fact that had no visible effect on Colby at all.

Colby picked up the cup of coffee Mrs. Butler had poured for her earlier and added sugar and milk to her taste. She stirred it thoughtfully and then walked over to the window to look outside. Jase realized she had turned her back deliberately and his face darkened. If she thought Mrs. Butler's presence would give her immunity, he was just about to dispel that comforting fiction, he thought savagely.

"I noticed that you haven't begun unpacking yet, Colby." Jase broke the palpable silence. "You have about a half an hour before lunch. I'm sure you could make a good start in that length of time."

The naked command in his voice caused Mrs. Butler's jaw to drop. She'd never heard Jase use that tone, least of all to a woman, and to a young, sweet girl. . . . She shook her head in dismay. Something was very wrong between these two young people.

Colby whirled and confronted Jase, chin obstinately high and eyes sparkling. "I had hoped it wasn't going to be necessary, Jase." She drawled his name insultingly. "I thought you might have come to your senses overnight and be prepared to take me back or at least take me to the nearest place where I can command some public transport. You must realize you can't force me to stay here. You *mustn't!*" Some of the desperation she was feeling echoed in her voice, and the gesture she made was unconsciously pleading. "Jase, you don't realize what is at stake. Please believe me, I *must* go back! The job I'm doing depends on it. I—I promise I won't implicate you. Just let me go!"

For a moment the pleading was wiped away and naked fury flared in her face. "My father had no right, no right at all. I'll never forgive him for this!"

Jase's face had been steadily darkening as she spoke, and when she paused for breath, his face was almost black with rage. Margy Butler was watching them with dropped jaw and complete bewilderment.

"Colby!" Jase yelled. "Get upstairs and unpack your

66

things. You're here and here you'll stay until I say you can go. Resign yourself to that, young lady."

Colby held her ground and Jase advanced on her, prepared to pick her up bodily and carry her upstairs. They had both forgotten about Mrs. Butler, so intent were they on their private confrontation of wills. Mrs. Butler's shocked voice stopped Jase in his tracks as he was reaching for Colby, who had her arm cocked to heave her half-full coffee cup at his head.

"Jase Culhane, leave that girl alone. Colby, put down that cup! Don't you dare throw it at him." The sharp command effectively froze both combatants in their places. "I want to know exactly what's going on between you two. Have you had a sweetheart's quarrel or something? Jase, I'm ashamed of you, treating a guest in your house this way." She stood eyeing them sternly, arms folded across her chest, foot tapping in impatience.

Colby laughed sharply. "A guest in his house? Ho, ho, what a laugh!"

"Colby!" Jase's warning exclamation cracked the air.

"I'm no guest!" Colby yelled in fury. "He kidnapped me. He dragged me on his airplane and flew me off to God-knows-where and he's holding me here against my will!" she continued bitterly. "He and my darling daddy are in cahoots. I was tricked into coming to the airport, and your precious Jase abducted me. He could go to jail for last night's work. He could, and so could Davis and what's-his-name, and even my darling daddy who masterminded this whole idiotic scheme. And I'm getting mad enough to see that maybe you all will," she finished angrily.

"Whew," commented Mrs. Butler mildly. "And just how much of this is true, Jase?"

"All of it," he snapped, his patience totally gone. "Her father wanted her brought here to get her away from the wild crowd she was associating with. I brought her here, and here she'll stay, until her father tells me to bring her back. Is that clear, Margy? You're not to aid and abet her in any way. This is for her own good, and you'll allow me and her father to be the judges of what's best for her."

Margy Butler looked from one furious face to the other and something twinkled deep in the back of her eyes. She'd known Jase, man and boy, and his behavior with this slender, fiery girl was so out of character for him that she nearly laughed aloud. *If I hadn't stopped him, I really think he might have tossed her over his shoulder caveman style,* she chuckled internally. *Of course he might have got a coffee cup smack between the eyes before he managed it. I think Colby can be counted on to hold her own against Jase, and I never thought to see a woman I could say that about. Best leave the two of them to fight it out . . . I can see that it doesn't come to actual bloodshed.*

Besides, the girl's got honest eyes. She's a good girl, in spite of what he's been told about her. It'll be interesting to watch him find that out for himself. She felt a stirring of interest she hadn't felt since her daughter and son-in-law were killed. *I think Colby's going to be good for us all,* she concluded happily. *Her coming has certainly put life into the place. I wonder if Jase is going to be able to stand the strain. Wait until the boys get a look at her.*

Aloud she said only, "I'll leave it to you and Colby to decide when she's to go back, Jase. Paul and I will move into the big house, though. I plan to be here to see that no blood flows, and it's better if Colby has another woman in the house." She turned back to the mound of dough and began to knead it. "Colby, Jase is right. You have time to start unpacking before lunch. Lay the things that need ironing on your bed and we'll get to them later. If you need more hangers, there are some in the linen closet in the bathroom."

Colby went out the door without another word. Jase started to follow her and Margy said sharply, "Jase, leave the girl alone. If you haven't anything outside to do, go set the table. Both of you need time to cool off."

Jase muttered something beneath his breath, but he didn't attempt to follow Colby. He didn't go in to set the table either. He stomped out the back door and just missed slamming it behind him. Margy grinned. Jase was not a man who took kindly to being thwarted.

She'd seen him grow up. Her husband had worked for Jase's father and the two families had been friends. When Jase had bought the ranch, a year after her husband's death from a heart attack, Jase offered her the job of housekeeper. She had been bored and welcomed the congenial job to supplement her pensions. She was trained for nothing save domestic work, but she was a marvelous homemaker. She had made Jase very comfortable, adding a little extra mothering when she thought he needed it, but she never forgot that he was the boss. She had never presumed, on the strength of their family friendship, to attempt to exert any authority over him—not that it would've been possible anyway, she chuckled. Jase radiated a natural authority; he had even as a young boy.

He generally knew what he wanted and got it. He was a hard worker and a fair man. His men worked willingly for him and he never had trouble finding temporary help when necessary, the mark of a good man to work for in these parts. He was also stubborn and he had a black temper when crossed about something he really wanted.

He was also unused to having a pretty young girl tell him where to get off. The girls around here considered Jase the apple on the top of the tree and waited hopefully for him to fall into their laps. To be fair, he was no womanizer, but it wasn't for lack of opportunity. Margy had always privately thought that Jase would never be permanently attracted to a girl unless she could match him for strength of character. She wouldn't presume to judge the depth of Colby's character on such short acquaintance, but Colby sure could match him for temper! Margy attacked the waiting dough with renewed vigor.

Colby stormed up the stairs to her room and shut the door behind her with a small slam. She also locked it firmly and then stood in the middle of the room breathing heavily through her temper-pinched nostrils. Jase Culhane was the absolute, the living end! She'd get Matt to put him in jail for the rest of his natural life, and her father in an adjoining cell. How dare they do this to her! She could scream; she could pound her head against the wall, or better yet, Jase's head. She stood motionless for perhaps five minutes until her temper cooled enough for rational thought, and then she began to plan.

First of all, she needed to know where she was. It was ridiculous not to even know what state one was in. Then she needed to know how far the nearest town was, and if there was a road leading to it. What form of communication did the ranch have with the outside world? They couldn't be totally cut off. . . . A phone perhaps, or even a radio? They had to get supplies from somewhere, and who and where were the nearest neighbors? Mrs. Butler wasn't going to actively help her get away. She had already opted out of that in deference to Jase, but she wasn't actively hostile. Maybe Colby could at least get her to tell her some of the things she needed to know.

That meant, Colby realized with dismay, that she had to go back downstairs for lunch and, while she was eating, she must refrain from heaving the nearest solid object at the head of one Jase Culhane. And he hadn't even had the courtesy to tell her his last name, Colby fumed, chalking up just one more black mark against Jase's overloaded record.

She still couldn't bring herself to begin unpacking. It was somehow an admission of defeat. She'd live out of suitcases if she had to. She was not going to unpack her clothes and hang them up in the closets of Jase Culhane's house.

She spent the time before lunch washing out the panty hose and briefs she had worn yesterday in the washbasin of the bathroom. She draped them over a handy towel rack. Jase would probably raise his bachelor's eyebrows in horror, she thought with great satisfaction. Maybe she should drape them over his shaving mirror, but she'd seen no signs that he used this bathroom. Perhaps the master bedroom had its own bath attached.

With slightly increased heart rate and a militant sparkle in her eye, she went downstairs. Since she didn't know the rest of the layout of the house and was determined not to be caught exploring, she went to the only room she knew, the kitchen. Mrs. Butler was there, ladling a delicious-smelling stew into a large serving dish. A large bowl of mixed tossed salad and a platter of fresh corn were ready to be carried to the table. Colby found, upon investigation, that a covered basket held still-warm bread.

'The dining room is through that door, Colby. We'll eat in there since we're having the main meal at noon. Would you carry some of this food through and I'll call the men." Mrs. Butler was calmly matter-of-fact.

Colby picked up the salad and the bread and went to the door indicated. It was slightly ajar and she pushed it open with her hip. She found a table set with four places, grouped at one end of the long table. The chairs were of beautifully carved black walnut, and from what she could see of the legs of the table beneath the crisp snow-white tablecloth, the table and eight chairs were part of a set. A buffet, graceful for all its size, and a china cabinet were of the same rich wood and bore the same carving. The chandelier that glittered above the table was crystal or she had never seen crystal before. *Lord, I'd hate to have to dust that*, she thought irreverently. Mrs. Butler maintains a high standard, she realized. She wondered if they ate breakfast amid all this magnificence. If so, it had to be eggs Benedict. Plebeian cornflakes just wouldn't have cut it.

She went back into the kitchen for the deep bowl of stew and found Jase there. He was dressed as he had been during their earlier confrontation, in jeans and work shirt, with battered riding boots on his feet, but he had washed his face and slicked a comb through his damp hair. When she started to pick up the heavy bowl of stew, Jase forestalled her. "I'll do that. It's too heavy for you to carry. You bring in the corn and the milk jug." He suited action to words and lifted the heavy bowl easily, carrying it into the dining room and setting it down on the waiting hot trivet. He then held the door back for her while she brought in the corn and the frosted jug of milk that had been set on the counter. She thanked him for the courtesy with an impersonal nod and he smiled tightly.

"You're welcome, Colby," he said, mocking her silence, and she shot him a blue-eyed glare. "The milk is from the house cow," he went on to inform her, "and may be a bit rich to your palate if you're used to skimmed. We don't separate the cream. If you'd prefer, there's iced tea or fruit juice, or even water. It's from a well and may taste a little strange to you at first since it's not loaded with chlorine and other noxious chemicals, but it's probably the cleanest water you've ever had."

"I'll have milk, thank you," she said politely and her voice had the distant, chill quality of a breeze blowing down from a snow-topped mountain slope, the subtle icy intonation one might use to assure an importunate waiter that one does not really desire a second cup of coffee, but would appreciate rendering of the bill. Dismissive.

Jase's black brows drew down in a thunderous frown and then, as if by magic, a thought seemed to amuse him, and he chuckled in appreciation. *Show your claws all you want, little kitten. I think you'll find I've blunted their little needle points most satisfactorily.* He began to pour milk into three of the four waiting glasses. The fourth was already filled with water.

Colby watched him suspiciously but he went about his self-imposed task with unconcern, a maddening smile at some private thought playing about his hateful mouth. She considered kicking him in the shins again—she was sure she could, with careful aim, hit the same place she had the night before—but regretfully decided that he'd certainly be alert for such a move and would probably dodge her easily.

He might look totally relaxed, but she noticed that he took care never to unbalance as he leaned over to pour the milk. He kept an unobtrusive, wary eye on her and she decided snidely that she wouldn't risk giving him the satisfaction of kicking at him and missing. If she swung on him again, she wanted to connect.

There was something about this man that affected her so . . . physically. She hadn't hit a male in anger since nursery school, but since she'd met Jase she'd done her best to commit mayhem upon his person so many times in less than twenty-four hours that she'd lost count. It wasn't like her. It worried her. Why should the fact that he'd looked her up and down and judged her of doubtful morals when he first laid eyes on her back at the airport infuriate her so? She had thought she looked like a tramp herself—it was part of her job—and it had never bothered her before because she really didn't care what was thought of her as long as she, herself, was satisfied with her standard of behavior.

But this man's misjudgment rankled. She had even caught herself thinking childishly, *Someday he'll find out what I'm really doing and then he'll be sorry for misjudging me. So there!*

Ridiculous. She was just furious because he had dared to kidnap her. That was what made her react so violently to him! Nothing else! And she'd show him. She'd get away, in spite of all he could do to keep her. So there! She laughed quietly to herself. Jase shot her a very suspicious look.

"What are you planning now, you young devil?" he questioned her rhetorically, not expecting any answer.

"Just what I have been since I first laid eyes on you," she answered him with sweet malice. "How to get as far away from you as I can."

His eyebrows snapped back down into a black line and he started toward her with no innocent intent. Inwardly she quailed, but she didn't retreat. She faced him with defiant bravado and an unwillingly admiring spark gleamed in his silver eyes. Colby didn't know what would have happened just then had not a most timely interruption occurred.

Mrs. Butler pushed open the door between the dining room and the kitchen and summed up the position of the two antagonists at a glance. Resignedly she said, "Are you two at it again? Honestly, you both remind me of a pair of nursery-school children, forever squabbling. I insist on a truce for the duration of the meal at least. Perhaps a good meal will sweeten both your tempers." She didn't sound as though she held out any great hopes for that eventuality however.

Colby asked, with as much poise as she could muster under the circumstances, "Does anything else need to be put on the table? We've"—she choked slightly on the word—"brought in everything that was sitting ready."

Margy swept a considering eye across the table. "No, everything's on except the honey and the butter, but Paul's bringing them in with him."

The door opened just on cue and a thin, colt-gangly young man came in with the items clutched in his outsize hands. His face was too thin, almost gaunt, and he dragged his left leg slightly, but his eyes were bright and intelligent. He looked at Colby and Jase, still facing each other with obvious tension. His eyes swept back to Colby and widened with unmistakable appreciation. A low, totally masculine whistle pursed his lips and he grinned.

"I must say, Jase, when you kidnap a girl, you sure do pick a smasher. If I were you, I'd just forget about ransom and keep her instead." He walked on to the table and put down the crock of honey and the butter he'd brought in.

Jase burst out laughing at Colby's astounded expression. To Paul he said, "Ah, but you see, nobody's willing to pay me anything to bring her back. In fact they want me to keep her. Kidnapping is no longer a money-making proposition, I'm afraid."

Paul pulled out a chair on the side of the table nearest the door and helped his grandmother to be seated. Jase took Colby's arm at the elbow and directed her around to the opposite side of the table, performing the same courteous service for her. Then he and Paul took their own seats, Jase at the head of the table, with Colby on his right and Paul next to his grandmother, who sat on Jase's left.

Before he began serving, Jase smiled down at Colby. "As you may have gathered, Colby, this young man is Paul Stoneman, Margy's grandson." His eyes twinkled as he nodded toward Paul. "Paul knows all about you, Colby," Jase said significantly. "I told him you are a most unwilling guest, but that we're going to do our best to make your stay with us an interesting one."

He began to ladle out the stew. Colby looked down at the plateful he had given her. There was just room for one ear of corn. The stew filled the rest of the space. She was hungry, but *that* hungry? After the first bite of the gravy-rich meat, she decided she was, after all, that hungry. She wasn't sure just what seasonings Mrs. Butler had mixed and mingled in the stew, but it was delicious. Besides the usual carrots and potatoes and cubed beef, there were also fresh mushrooms, little pearl onions, and celery, and the crisp green salad was another meal in itself.

She watched in amazement as Jase and Paul both polished off second helpings of everything the same size as their first. There hadn't been much conversation during the meal itself, merely an occasional laconic "Pass the salt, please" or a "More bread, Jase?" from Mrs. Butler, but that had suited Colby just fine.

She had been deep in consideration of the surprising fact that Jase had evidently decided to admit freely to Paul (and whom else?) that he had kidnapped her. He didn't seem at all worried by possible implications or legal ramifications. Was he depending on a presumed unwillingness on her part to subject her own father to public prosecution? And yet, that didn't quite fit in, because a person capable of the type of behavior Jase obviously considered her capable of wouldn't stick at making a whopping scandal. It was almost as though he knew she had no grounds for legal action, as if her father had the right to send her whither and when he would. And that didn't make sense either, because she was her own mistress and had been since she reached her majority.

Jase finished the last bite of stew and leaned back in his chair. "That was delicious, Margy. It's really a crime to call that a plain stew. It deserves the continental term "ragout" to indicate its superiority to humble stew. It's a good thing I'm not taking Merlin out far today. He'd toss me off for making him carry an overload."

"Oh, you are riding out this afternoon?" Margy responded. "Jim wanted to talk to you about something. He came by this morning before you were up. He said he'd be back in midafternoon."

Jase frowned slightly. "I hope we're still not having trouble with that pack of dogs. They pulled down a couple of calves over by Three Mile Creek last week, but I sent Donny and Carl out to track them down. Told 'em not to come back in until they'd accounted for the whole pack."

Colby hadn't been paying much attention to the rest of Jase's conversation with Margy. He was going away from the house. Now was the time to search and find the answers to a few questions, like "Where am I?" and "Where's the phone?"

"Well, I won't be far from the house," Jase said. "Colby has assured me that she isn't afraid of horses so I thought I'd give her a riding lesson. We don't want her to get bored so early in her visit."

Colby's head whipped up in shock. Jase's face was bland and guileless, but there was a certain gleam deep in his eyes. He was up to something. She knew it.

Jase was. He figured that if she was stiff and sore from a riding lesson she wouldn't be any too eager to try hiking to the nearest civilization, which was over forty miles away. Teaching her to ride had its drawbacks too, because a horse would make her mobile, but as long as he could keep her from finding out what direction to be mobile in. . . . Besides, he owed her something for that kick in the shins, and since spanking her directly had proved hazardous, he might just let one of his horses do it for him!

"I—I don't think I care to ride today," Colby said rather faintly. She wanted nothing more than a few hours alone in the house, free from the fear of running into Jase while she did a little genteel snooping.

Jase spoke with maddening reassurance. "I'll pick you out a very gentle horse, Colby. There's nothing to be afraid of and," he said, grinning devilishly, "we'll only ride over soft ground so you'll bounce if you do fall off."

"I don't want to ride!" she snapped, seeing her opportunity going glimmering.

"You're going to if I have to strap you in the saddle!" Jase retorted, his temper rising.

"Here they go again," Mrs. Butler said to Paul in a loud

aside. Jase and Colby ignored all distractions, intent as they were on glaring at each other.

Paul decided to add his bit. "You know, I always thought an abductee was supposed to be afraid of the abductor. Do you think Jase hasn't had enough practice at being a kidnapper?"

Jase stopped glaring at Colby and glared instead at Margy and Paul. Paul gulped. "I think I'll get back to my school lessons, Grandma. May I be excused?" At her smiling nod he rose hastily from the table. He scooped up his dirty plates and silverware and with a "See you later, Colby" disappeared into the kitchen.

Margy was made of sterner stuff. She finished her slice of bread with honey on it and said, "Before you go outside, Colby, I could use a hand with the dishes. Paul usually helps me, but . . ." She smiled.

"Of course, Mrs. Butler," Colby agreed with alacrity, and began to carry the used plates into the kitchen.

When Colby was in the other room, Margy admonished Jase, "Now, Jase, maybe she really isn't interested in riding. Are you sure she isn't afraid of horses?"

"That girl isn't afraid of the devil himself," Jase grunted. "She just wants to do anything she can to annoy me. Besides, she was hoping for a chance to snoop around the house without my catching her. By the way, I've taken all the phones on jacks out of the bedrooms. The only operative one in the house is the one in my study and my study will be locked. I'll give you a key, in case the phone rings or there's an emergency, but you'll have to promise not to let Colby in there. It's important, Margy. I don't want her getting the chance to go back any time soon. Her father was very emphatic about the crowd she was going around

79

with. They were no good . . . lots of drug users and burnouts. I won't have her go back to that sort of life!"

Margy wisely didn't comment on his vehemence. Jase might not want Colby to go back to her old associations, but Margy was beginning to suspect that perhaps Jase just didn't want her to go back!

Colby and Margy dealt with the dishes in harmony, chatting as they worked. Margy tossed out several promising and provocative subjects but Colby kept to generalities, and Margy was left, at the end, knowing no more of the inner Colby than she had before.

At last Colby could delay no longer. She understood Jase too well to think he would not be waiting for her, determined to enforce his dominance. She'd just have to make other opportunities, and a possibility was already formulating in her agile mind. She hadn't had formal police training, but Matt had put her through a couple of crash courses, one of which might come in handy in the present situation. She'd have to think about it. In any event there was obviously going to be no way to avoid the riding lesson, much as she'd like to. Jase wanted her in the saddle, so in the saddle she'd go. She hoped it made him happy.

Jase had been busy while Colby had been drying dishes. He'd gone back up to her room and found her unpacking in the same state as last time he'd looked. That was another battle she was going to lose, he vowed. He knew very well why she was resisting taking even so much as one dress out of the suitcase to hang on a hanger. She not only fought him on the big things, she was determined to oppose him on the small as well. He wondered where she found her energy.

He went back downstairs and stuck his head in the

kitchen door. Colby was shaking out the dish towel and hanging it on the drying rack. He enjoyed the sight of her trim figure and that obstinate little spine and her chuckle as she and Margy exchanged some quip. He frowned at the stiffening of her whole body when he spoke, but some-day . . . he vowed!

"Margy, I'd like a word with you before Colby and I go out, please."

He drew Margy after him into the hall, leaving the door slightly ajar so that he could keep an eye on Colby. He didn't trust her an inch. Colby unconcernedly began to massage hand lotion into her hands.

"Margy, while we're out, I want you to go to Colby's room and unpack every shoe and stitch of clothing we brought with us. When that's done, get Paul to take the suitcases to the storage room. I'd like Colby settled in for a long stay by the time we finish our riding lesson." Jase smiled in happy anticipation of the success of this latest ploy.

"Heating up the conflict, Jase?" Margy questioned him dryly, her own eyes twinkling in appreciation.

"D'you think it needs 'heating up'?" he chuckled. "I thought it was burning nicely all on its own. This is just one small engagement, but I'm going to win the war as well."

"No wonder your mother always called you a limb of Satan when you were little, Jase. All right, I'll unpack Colby for you."

"Thanks, Margy." Jase went into the kitchen where Colby unwillingly waited. Margy watched the two of them from the doorway and thought how well matched they were physically. Colby's black head came just below Jase's chin, and though he towered over her, somehow he didn't

81

dwarf her. The breadth of his shoulders was a pleasing contrast to Colby's lithe woman-fragility, fragile only in contrast, however, to the masculine bone and bulk. The proud lift of her chin and the collected grace of all her movements bespoke the fact that she stood on her own feet. She'd be a partner, never a clinging vine needing to be tenderly nurtured against the storms of life, not a few of which would be of her own making. Trouble and Colby seemed to be natural acquaintances, Margy mused.

"Shall we go now, Colby?" Jase asked, but the look in his eyes said it was a command, not a request.

Colby squared her shoulders and tilted her chin at a determined angle. "If I must," she agreed. "You—you won't put me up on a horse that bucks, will you, Jase?" Her voice had a slight quaver, and she watched his reaction from beneath her long eyelashes.

His hard face softened slightly. "You'll be fine, Colby," he assured her soothingly. "I won't let any harm come to you. We'll start slowly. I'll even put your horse on a leading rein at first, if it'll make you feel better."

Her lips quivered slightly, but Jase was opening the back door and missed that slight betraying sign. "No, I guess I'd better do this properly from the start." Colby rejected his offer quietly. "Animals sense when you're afraid of them, don't they? I wouldn't want my horse to get the wrong idea about me."

"I don't believe you're afraid of anything, Colby," Jase said indulgently, as they went out the back door.

"Oh, yes, Jase. There are lots of things I'm afraid of. Any sensible person is. I'm not foolhardy by any means. Matt says that a man who says he's not afraid of anything is either a fool or dead, and if he's that big a fool, he'll soon *be* dead." Colby had forgotten for just that moment to whom she was speaking, and so she spoke naturally and unguardedly. She regretted it almost immediately.

Jase grabbed her shoulders and spun her to face him. "Who is Matt? What is he to you, that you quote him with such authority?" Unconsciously he started to shake her again. The mention of that name enraged him. It had been this Matt she had called on the phone, the man she had turned to for rescue when she was abducted.

A low, menacing concert of growls interrupted him. He had forgotten the two dogs waiting for him outside. Kelpie and Lije, his blue heelers, had been waiting patiently outside the kitchen door and had fallen into pace with the couple as they came outside. Now they were reacting to the simmering antagonism. He released Colby's shoulders abruptly and she staggered back slightly. The two dogs closed in on either side of her and Jase opened his mouth to order them back from her, but his mouth stayed open in shock.

The two dogs were not menacing Colby. They had closed protectively beside her and now flanked her, looking balefully up at him. Colby knelt in the dirt beside them and placed an arm around each hackled neck. She spoke soothingly, liltingly, to each animal, stroking their flattened ears until the coiled tension left their bodies and their ears pricked again. The dogs butted gently against her and their tails began to wag with puppyish enthusiasm. They whined and wriggled adoringly against her, and Lije so far forgot himself as to roll over and present his stomach to be rubbed. Colby laughingly complied, briefly, and then rose back to her feet, snapping her fingers in command. The dogs immediately came to attention, watching her intently for her slightest motion that would tell them what their goddess desired next.

"It's a gift from my great-great-grandmother on my mother's side," she explained nonchalantly. "Dogs and small children love me. Family legend has it that she was a witch, and I look just like a miniature we have of her. It can be a nuisance at times but it also has its uses, wouldn't you agree?"

Jase was still looking at his dogs. They were watching Colby, quivering eagerly.

"What are their names, Jase?" Colby asked.

"Kelpie," Jase said, pointing to the larger male, "and Lije." He indicated the smaller, younger male. The dogs flicked an ear back as he spoke their names but didn't remove their attention from Colby.

Colby knelt before the dogs again, placing one hand under each chin, looking into the eyes of each dog in turn. They went rock still. "Kelpie, Lije. Go to Jase. Mind Jase. Good dogs." She scratched each briefly and stood up again. The dogs wheeled and returned to sit beside Jase, one to a side, now waiting for his command.

"Thank you," he said dryly. "Do we have to do this with all the dogs on the place?"

"It might be a good idea, if I'm liable to come into contact with them while they're working. Once it's done, they won't come to me except on my specific command or if they judge me in danger." Colby spoke with utmost seriousness, and Jase looked at her sharply. She smiled angelically back.

"Have you ever been to a dog show?" he asked, only half joking.

"Good Lord, no!" she shuddered.

They started walking again and Colby looked around her appreciatively. The land was lush and green out past the immediate area of the environs of the ranch buildings.

They seemed to be in a large valley, or at least, she amended, she could see mountains rising in the distance on two sides of her. Clumps of trees dotted the immediate area, but not being country-oriented, she recognized only a few varieties. The air was clear and clean and she breathed deeply in appreciation. A faint breeze lifted tendrils of her hair, bringing with it a faint tang of pine and horse, intermingled.

As they neared some stables and corrals a man came out leading two horses, already saddled and bridled. The larger of the two, a magnificently muscled quarter horse stallion danced restively and mouthed his bit. He was a gleaming dark chestnut with a narrow blaze running between his eyes to taper down to nothing before it reached his muzzle. The mare who flanked him was a quarter horse too but of daintier build and lighter color. She stood quietly, head up and ears pricked inquiringly.

Another breeze gusted between the horses and approaching couple, and Jase watched resignedly as each horse's head came up and nostrils expanded, questing. They took urgent steps toward Jase and Colby, necks stretching eagerly, nearly jerking the reins from the hands of the man holding them.

"Let 'em go, Mark," Jase called, and Mark obeyed, looping the reins back over their heads and releasing the pulling horses.

Jase watched Colby brace herself as the two horses approached at a half trot, sliding to a stop before her and nuzzling into her chest. Mark watched openmouthed and Jase knew just how he felt.

" 'Animals sense when you're afraid of them, don't they?' " he quoted ironically. "Are we going to have every horse and cow on the place following us around, Colby?"

85

She had the grace to blush. "Well, I haven't had much to do with cows," she said doubtfully. "I don't think they're as much affected, but the dogs can send them off if they bother us too much. The horses aren't as bad as the dogs, but they do tend to congregate, given the chance. You'll appreciate that in the city contact with more than the occasional mounted policeman's horse is rare. I've never been a 'guest' at a ranch before," she pricked delicately.

"Point taken. Your claws have sharpened back up again, kitten."

By this time Mark had arrived and his weathered countenance bore an expression of ludicrous amazement. The horses were still nuzzling Colby and she pushed them away with a laugh. "Give over, loves, do." She smiled up at Mark and held out her hand. "Hi, I'm Colby Duncan."

"She's a witch, Mark, holding power over man and beast," Jase interjected dryly. "This is Mark Farrell, Colby. I've told him that you are an . . . ah . . . unwilling guest. He won't help you either, nor will any of my other men, fascinate how you will."

Mark shuffled his feet in embarrassment, and Colby took pity on him. "I admire loyalty, Mark. Don't feel bad. We'll keep this disagreement between Mr. Culhane and myself. I won't ask you for what you can't give."

Jase ground his teeth as Mark smiled fatuously down at Colby. Just at that moment the mare, chaffing at being ignored, nosed into Colby's back and made her stagger slightly. Mark put out a hand to catch her, but Jase was quicker still. He caught her in his arms and held her against his body while she found her feet, holding her far longer and tighter than Colby thought the situation warranted. She wiggled slightly and Jase reluctantly released her.

It was unnerving, but Colby could still feel the hard lines of his body imprinted down the length of her side. She was blindingly conscious of the way his muscular forearm had rested just beneath her breasts, pressing upward into the soft fullness. He had only touched her in anger before. This time his touch held no anger, it held— what?

She turned back to the horse. "What's her name?" she queried Mark.

"Babe," he answered. "She's gentle and light-mouthed. You won't have any trouble with her, Colby." He chuckled. "But then I guess you wouldn't even if she wasn't."

Colby smiled back over her shoulder at him, spoke softly to the mare, and walked to her side. She gathered the reins competently, checked the tightness of the cinch, and swung up into the saddle. She stood briefly in the stirrups and shifted experimentally.

"Mark, this right stirrup is a bit too long. Would you move it up a notch for me, please?" She reined Babe around as she spoke and presented the off side of the horse to him, pulling her foot back out of the stirrup to facilitate his task.

While Mark was busy, Merlin nosed lovingly at Colby's left knee. She rubbed him absently behind the ears while she watched Mark work. The dogs whined jealously and Jase looked sourly at them.

"That better, Colby?" Mark asked.

She put her foot back in the stirrup again and stood once more. "Just fine, Mark. Thanks a lot."

"Ah, Colby," Mark said hesitantly. "Be careful with

those sneakers, huh? You really need some heeled boots so your foot doesn't get caught in the stirrup."

"I have some in the house, Mark. I'll wear them next time, but I don't think we'll be going far this time, will we, Mr. Culhane? I didn't know we were going riding this afternoon," she finished in explanation to Mark.

"No, we won't be going far," Jase said through clenched teeth. He swung up on Merlin and reined him back. Merlin seemed inclined to jib a bit until Colby kneed Babe forward to side him, whereupon he quieted immediately. Colby waved good-bye to the watching Mark and he lifted a hand in reply.

Jase opened the first gate they came to and Colby guided Babe through. They moved off when Jase had secured the gate once more and they rode silently side by side for a short space. Colby rode easily and relaxed in the saddle, her body gently adjusting to the motion of her horse.

"Ah," she sighed. "For pleasure and distance I do prefer a western saddle. Jumping's fun, but scenery watching is nice too."

"How long have you ridden?" Jase asked in a carefully neutral tone.

"Oh, we had lessons and gymkhanas at boarding school. I've been on a few hunts as well, but drags only. I don't approve of the real thing."

Jase made a muffled sound and Colby looked at him sidelong. "Well," she said reasonably, "you never *asked* if I could ride. It never pays to assume too much about people, Jase Culhane."

"Especially about you, eh, Colby?" he said ruefully. "You set me up and I gulped the bait beautifully. A leading rein . . ." He began to laugh.

Colby enjoyed the ride. It had been too long since she

had lived only in the present, not worrying about what was to come later. Since she had no choice anyway, she took a couple of hours out of time and refused to worry about any of her problems. She was to have this, Jase decreed it, so she set herself to enjoying it. That was easy. The land was lovely and Babe was a sweet mover, responsive and eager.

She forgot about Jase, except as another human being enjoying with her the freedom and speed of four powerful, distance-eating legs. By the time they cantered back to the main ranch, dogs panting at their horses' heels, her hair had broken free of the confining ponytails and streamed freely behind her.

Had the men watching their return been of poetical bent, they might have thought in terms of Diana riding to the hunt. As it was, they merely admired the way she sat a horse and the flushed and laughing beauty of her face. Jase's eyebrows drew into a mild scowl when he saw the number of men who had managed to find jobs in the immediate vicinity—there were a lot of saddles and other bits of equipment getting a lot of attention—but he said nothing for the moment. He, too, had been enjoying the truce, though he was too astute to think it could endure much longer.

He resignedly made the introductions and secretly enjoyed the startled expressions as the various dogs reacted to Colby's presence, ignoring their owners, as had Lije and Kelpie before them, until Colby sent them back to sit at their proper master's heels. Lije and Kelpie wore smug doggy expressions because they were allowed to sit near Colby. Jase stood at her side and so the dogs stuck closer than ticks to him.

Mark offered to care for Babe on Colby's behalf and led

her away as she nickered back over her shoulder. Jase retained Merlin for the moment, meaning to ride over to see his foreman, Jim, who had left several messages for him. He watched Colby charm his men, young and old, for as long as he could stand it, then scattered them and escorted Colby to the house. There he delivered her to Margy Butler. An exchange of significant looks with Margy assured him that Colby was now unpacked and settled in for the duration, and he went off to find his foreman, whistling cheerily as he swung back up into Merlin's saddle.

CHAPTER FOUR

Colby was depressed. The men had liked her and didn't seem inclined to judge her, no matter what Jase had told them about the reason she was an unwilling guest. It was equally clear, however, that they weren't prepared to help her if it meant going against Jase's orders. He must also have covered very thoroughly just what would be considered "helping" her because none of the men had let slip where she was in relation to any place else. She could steal a horse, even if she had to ride it bareback and bridleless, but she still had no idea where to ride. She could have the freedom of the ranch, but since it was measured in square miles rather than acres, that freedom wasn't going to do her a fat lot of good at the present.

There was nothing for it. She was just going to have to do a spot of snooping when the opportunity arose, and if it didn't arise, she'd just have to manufacture the chance —like after the witching hour. She'd have to become an inside cat burglar, not to put too nice a point on it! That meant a flashlight.

Colby and Margy were having a companionable cup of coffee when Paul came bounding in to ask for a snack and to question Colby interestedly about her effect on animals. He had heard the men marveling about their dogs' reactions to Colby and was agog for details. She explained again about her great-great-grandmother and admitted that a second cousin of her mother's was reputed to have the same empathy or attraction for animals as did Colby. Since the cousin lived on a sheep-raising station (ranch to Paul) in Australia and had had minimal contact with the rest of the family since she married forty years ago, Colby could not offer concrete substantiation of her own knowledge of this interesting bit of family lore.

Paul then wanted to know if she had any other hidden talents. Colby laughed and denied any ability to read minds or walk through solid walls. Paul was disappointed but bore up manfully.

Margy beamed at them both and told Colby to call her Margy instead of that overformal Mrs. Butler. Inwardly she was elated. She had known Colby was going to be good for them. Paul's laugh had been full throated and blithe, something she hadn't heard since the accident. With a shock she realized that Colby had been with them for something short of twenty-four hours and she'd turned them all upside down already.

Paul had lost that grief-old solemnness that sat ill on such a young boy. She, herself, was enjoying the novelty of another woman in the house and was, she admitted, deriving much secret amusement watching the sparks flare between Jase and Colby. And as for Jase, poor man, Margy suspected he was beginning to doubt whether he was on his head or his heels.

He had successfully managed to kidnap Colby, but keeping her—ah, that was proving to be an entirely different thing altogether. In Margy's shrewd estimation Colby was a lady, but she was far from being ladylike. She'd been near as not to heaving that coffee cup between Jase's eyes before Margy stepped in, and somehow Margy couldn't believe that that was a habit of Colby's. Nice girls—and anyone with a quarter of an eye could tell that Colby was a thoroughly nice girl—just didn't go around heaving cups at provoking men, even those who had kidnapped them at their father's behest.

Colby was thinking, *If I were a flashlight in this house, where would I be?* She was sure there had to be at least several. Every house needed some, and an isolated one more than most. She set about subtly questioning Margy.

She began, "I imagine living in such an isolated position makes for some very special housekeeping problems, food supplies, power, and such. I gather you generate your own power."

Margy was no fool, but she didn't see what harm a general discussion of the problems of isolated rural living would do. She amiably followed Colby's lead and gave her a thorough briefing on the adjustments that had to be made, of necessity, when one was so far from the nearest grocery store and doctor, not to mention entertainment.

Colby found it fascinating, in spite of herself, and even though much of it was not to her point of immediate concern, she listened with absorbed interest. While Margy had the most modern of appliances, thanks to the good offices of the electrical generator, there were also provisions for alternative heating, cooking, and lighting. Colby hoped her ears didn't prick too noticeably when Margy mentioned the last. Oh, so casually, and she hoped unobtrusively, with all the lightfooted delicacy of a cat stalking a blissfully unaware bird, Colby maneuvered Margy into showing her all these various provisions.

Bingo! Margy proudly displayed the wood-burning stoves, doubly useful for heating and cooking, and the oil and kerosene lamps, which could shed a soft, romantic, and, alas, rather smelly light when incandescent bulbs failed. There were boxes of candles, basic white through a range of colors and scents, and a burglar's dream of varieties of flashlights, ranging from small penlights up through powerful camplights. Colby mentally marked off a utilitarian D-cell flashlight that could be easily shielded but would still yield enough illumination for her purpose. She thought about attempting to purloin it on the spot, under Margy's nose as it were, but decided it would be safer to wait until later. She could always grope her way down to the pantry and find the flashlight by feel. In her mind she marked its location for later reference.

The next task was to get Margy to take her on a tour of the house. Margy was glad to comply. She wasn't really into the role of auxiliary jailer that Jase had thrust upon her, and the possibility that Colby might have ulterior motives behind her expressed interest in the house never crossed her mind. Jase wanted Colby kept busy and out of mischief. Margy didn't realize that Jase's idea of mischief might be considerably more comprehensive than Margy's.

After all, Colby had most forcefully brought home to Jase the depth of her desire to return to her former haunts. She had made that desire excruciatingly clear to him, and he would, rightly, have viewed her sudden interest in his house and its layout with justifiable suspicion. Jase, however, wasn't there. Margy was. Colby got her tour of the house, except for Jase's locked study, of course. Since that was the object of the exercise—a locked room was sure to contain just what she most wanted to see—Colby marked that particular room's location with considerable care on her mental map of the house floorplan.

After the tour of the downstairs was completed, Colby excused herself to go upstairs and remove the traces of horse she had acquired during her afternoon's outing. Margy let her go with a smile and kept an ear cocked for any reaction when Colby visited her room. It wasn't long in coming. A very audible "Dammit!" echoed down the stairs, followed by Colby's footsteps as she took the stairs back down two at a time. She stuck her head in the kitchen again and wailed, "Margy, how could you?" and didn't wait for a reply.

Colby was fuming again. It wasn't really Margy's fault, Colby knew. This was all Jase's doing, another round of one-upmanship, and she had to admit he had won this one hands down. Her suitcases were gone, so she couldn't repack them if she wanted to, but she wouldn't have, even were the suitcases still available. That would have been childish, and Colby recognized it. That involuntary wail to Margy would be her only reaction. She would preserve a dignified silence about the whole incident. It wouldn't recoup the position, but it wouldn't make it worse either.

Jase Culhane was a sneaky, unprincipled, arrogant, infuriating man! She'd get away from him or know the reason why!

Colby took a leisurely shower, washed her hair, and picked out a demure little dress calculated to make her look fragile, defenseless, and gorgeous, if she did say so herself. She had her own weapons to use on the likes of Jase Culhane and they didn't have to be tangible, like a coffee cup.

Thus it was that when Jase came through the kitchen late that afternoon he was greeted by the sight of Colby, daintily enveloped in an apron, dicing vegetables at the sink. The rapidity of her strokes with the knife and the precise evenness of the cubes she was turning out proved her to be no stranger to culinary accomplishments.

As he approached her a softly feminine fragrance drifted toward him, delicately wafting past his nostrils with teasing persistence. Her glossy black hair was piled softly atop her head with soft tendrils framing her ears and forehead, and he felt a sudden mad impulse to kiss the bared nape of her neck. The impulse died a sudden death when she looked up at him and he saw her eyes were a stormy blue, not a soft, inviting violet.

"Margy's fixing the rooms for herself and Paul. They've moved into the house for the time being. I offered to fix supper for us since she's had a lot of extra work thrust on her recently." Colby concentrated on her dicing again. It wouldn't do to cut one of her fingers. She'd need them all for what she had planned tonight.

Jase's lips twitched at her oblique reference to the success of his latest ploy. It obviously rankled badly, but she wasn't going to give him the satisfaction of referring to it directly. He considered mentioning it himself, but the flashing memory of the coffee cup decided him against it. He'd wait until she was holding something a little less lethal than a chef's knife.

He muttered something about cleaning up before supper and left the kitchen. Colby smiled nastily to herself. She'd seen his nostrils twitch as the perfume reached him. It had been a gift from her father on her twenty-first birthday, and at over a hundred dollars an ounce, it should have some effect. Of course, the impact of her dress had been somewhat blunted by the apron, but on the whole she was not ill pleased.

Hostilities resumed over supper, which they ate around the dining room table.

Jase had shaved and showered, and looked disturbingly handsome in dark slacks and an open-necked blue Qiana shirt. When he spread his warm hand over the soft, sensitive skin of the inside of her elbow to escort her to her chair, Colby felt her heart slam against her ribs. By a great effort of will she managed to keep herself from jerking her arm from his gentle clasp and thus betraying her agitation, but it was a near thing. She wasn't able to control the stiffening of her entire body from the shock his touch sent through her system, but she hoped he would attribute it to repugnance instead of to the true cause, which was her unexpected and unwelcome awareness of him as a handsome, virile man. It shook Colby no end.

She was doing just fine hating his guts. She didn't want any unwelcome responses complicating her already intricately tangled life. In spite of her less than salubrious surroundings while at work, she was basically inexperienced, and she planned to stay that way for the foreseeable future. The men with whom she was in daily contact had no appeal for her, making it easy to turn off their advances. Her boarding school had been one of the last bastions of noncoeducational schools of its type, and during her further schooling, no man had succeeded in even denting her heart slightly.

What a sour joke on her it would be if she found herself becoming sexually aware of, and what was worse, attracted to Jase Culhane! If he ever found out, he'd laugh himself silly. He thought she was a promiscuous, spoiled little rich bitch, out for kicks and thrills. He'd already made his opinion painfully (her buttocks gave a reminiscent twinge) clear. He might try to take what he thought she'd offered others, but it wouldn't mean more than that to him. No way!

This silent pep talk did her a world of good. She was able to meet Jase's sardonic glances throughout the meal with equanimity, and the verbal barbs flew thick and fast throughout the entire meal. From soup (a homemade chicken vegetable that was a specialty of Colby's) through nuts (on top of the chocolate-chip cookies she had baked for a light dessert), Margy's and Paul's heads swiveled between the two verbal antagonists with the monotonous regularity of onlookers at a particularly rapid-volley tennis match.

Jase complimented Colby on the meal she had prepared, but his obvious amazement at her expertise in the kitchen made her long to throw the soup tureen at him, or at least dump it over his head. It wasn't *what* he said, it was *how* he said it! It wasn't until the meal was over that she realized that Jase had been deliberately provocative and he had thoroughly been enjoying her rapid rise to each temptingly dangled bit of bait. She'd been "led down the garden path" and she'd charged right down it like a bull with its eyes tightly closed. The look she gave him after this realization would have singed the eyelashes off of a fly at fifty paces. It was his turn to smile seraphically at her.

Suddenly they both began to laugh. Much as she might wish to, Colby just couldn't help herself. He had paid her back royally for the dogs and the horses. Honors even, and after her foray tonight, perhaps the balance would begin to tip in her favor. Colby had always been able to take a joke, even when the tables were turned on her, and she and Jase finally quit laughing in the closest they had come to harmony since their first stormy meeting. Margy and Paul regarded them with bewilderment, sending Jase and Colby off into another peal of laughter.

Jase and Paul helped clear the table, and while Colby

and Margy dealt with the dishes, Jase helped Paul with some of his math. With a patience Colby could only admire, Jase went over and over one particular difficult area until he was sure Paul was firmly grounded in the principle.

It's only with me that he has such a short fuse, Colby decided, conveniently forgetting her own responsibilities in setting off the various explosions that had dotted their relationship to date. Not that a halo of self-conscious rectitude floated over her head, for Colby was all too aware of her own shortcomings, but she considered herself the injured party. After all, she was the abductee and that should entitle her to some latitude!

After the last dish was dried and the last algebra problem mastered, Paul went off to prepare for bed. His elders adjourned to the living room, where Jase showed Colby the intricacies of his stereo set and allowed her to look through the contents of his cassette and record collections.

Colby asked guilelessly for a newspaper to read and Jase laughed. "You never give up, do you, Colby? No newspaper. Come with me and we'll find you something to read from the library—a nice history or an edifying biography perhaps." He held out a hand and hauled her to her feet from the floor where she sat going through records.

Colby came lithely to her feet, trying hard to maintain an impassive face as strange sensations rioted through her body. Jase didn't relinquish his hold on her hand as she had expected, but his touch was impersonal—no increased pressure or caressing movements of the thumb that curled around the back of her hand—so Colby didn't pull away. It didn't occur to her that the impersonality might be deliberate on Jase's part for that very reason.

With rare docility she followed him into the book-lined

room. Before he released her to find a book, they stood before the partially completed jigsaw puzzle that lay spread out on a sturdy wooden game table. It was an octagonal; she could tell because all of the edge pieces had been fitted into place. The pattern of the puzzle seemed to be composed solely of pinecones, interspersed here and there with occasional pine needles and bits of stick and dried leaves. It was a pretty picture and the soft blue shades and tones were pleasing. It would also be very difficult to complete since pinecones are not distinctive en masse.

As is often the way, her hand went directly to a piece that seemed to fit just there and slotted it into place. She stood for five minutes after that trying one piece after another and never found a one to fit. Jase in his turn found one piece, and no more.

"That's how it goes," he said philosophically. "I think that's how this puzzle will eventually be completed, one piece at a time, and only one per customer. Paul is the only one of us who has the patience to work on it after his beginner's luck has worn out. Most of us—everyone who comes into the library—usually give it five minutes at the outside. I think the record is held by Jim, my foreman, who found three pieces in a row, but I don't think he's found one since."

Colby chuckled. "He used up all his luck at once?" she said as she looked over the room.

"Something like that," Jase agreed.

The library was a cozy room. Three walls held bookshelves, mostly filled, with both hardbacks and paperbacks, a series of *National Geographic*s, plus several stacks of other magazines. At a cursory glance, there seemed to be everything ranging from light fiction, through biographies, weighty reference tomes, and all types of nonfiction. It was a serviceable, well-used collection, able to cater to a wide variety of needs and tastes, something very necessary in this isolated position.

The fourth wall held a series of paneled floor-to-ceiling cabinets, and she eyed them speculatively. She hadn't had a chance to explore earlier when Margy had been taking her on the tour of the house, but . . . Jase grinned, obviously reading her mind with consummate ease. He walked over to the cabinets and opened several of the doors wide.

"Help yourself," he drawled, and stood back to give her easy access.

"Thank you, but I'm not in the mood for games," she drawled right back, because the cabinets were filled with games, boxes of jigsaw puzzles, what looked like enough art and craft materials to stock a bazaar, and other useful, but to Colby useless, odds and ends.

Jase shut the doors with a mock regretful sigh. "What a pity. I was sure you'd be good at games."

These persistent double entendres were going to get out of hand any minute, Colby thought to herself. Jase was being deliberately provocative, and if he wasn't careful, he might get more of a rise from her than he had bargained for. It had been several hours since she had tried to hit him with something hard, but the urge was rising minute by minute. Colby wasn't all that hipped on self-control anyway when it came to Jase Culhane.

"Oh, I'm very good at games, Jase," she said through clenched teeth. "But I like to play them by my rules."

Jase moved toward Colby. She didn't like the gleam in his eyes. Pride forbade that she turn and run like a hunted hare, but her mouth suddenly went dry and she could feel a pulse in her throat start skipping and throbbing just

101

beneath the thin skin of her neck. Jase's eyes went unerringly to that subtle betrayer and she just stopped herself from clapping a hand over her throat.

He was very near now, and as he spoke softly he stretched out his hand and laid a finger over that vulnerable spot. "What rules do you play the game by, Colby?" The finger began to move gently, a butterfly-light touch. He traced the length of her neck from jawline to hollow where it met her shoulder.

His voice was very tranquil, very soft, and coaxing. Colby's eyes fluttered shut and she concentrated on the feel of that one warm finger, stroking, stroking the line of her throat. When Jase's hands cupped her jaw and tilted her face up, her eyes stayed shut. It was no surprise to feel his warm breath ghosting over her mouth, a precursor to the feel of his firm mouth teasing her lips. His kiss was not tentative, but it was gentle, wooing.

No contact except those soothing hands and that softly questing mouth, kissing hers from corner to corner. He deepened the pressure slowly, asking, not demanding, that she open to him. Where force would have got him nothing but a lacerated lip, tender care gave him the entry he sought. The kiss deepened, intensified, but still there was that dreamy, enchanted, timeless quality.

Jase brought the kiss to an end slowly, delicately, and began to trace the planes of her face with his mouth. He kissed the closed lids, the corners of her eyes, her forehead, and cheeks, learning with his mouth the contours of her face as a blind man might learn them with his fingers. Colby's heart rate had slowed to a heavy throbbing beat, and her hands, which had hung at her sides, began to move slowly, coming up to sightlessly seek the broad spread of his chest.

Before her hands could make contact with him though, he lifted his mouth away from her face slightly and still in that soothing, calm tone said, "Does Matt play by your rules, Colby? Who is he and what is he to you? Tell me, Colby, tell me, dear Colby."

Strange that that warm, sweet breath ghosting over her skin could leave such an icy cold trail behind it. It had taken a moment for her bemused mind to assimilate the sense of that deeply whispered collection of sounds, but after they formed themselves into coherent words, she came out of enchantment with a jolt.

Her eyes flew open to meet Jase's silvery ones inches away. He watched in fascination as the soft violet-blue so close to his changed and darkened into a stormy blue. When the wide open lids began to narrow down into fighting slits, his instinctive reflexes took over and he began to move back out of range.

He was almost quick enough, but his absorption with the phenomenon of the color change in her eyes slowed him just that fraction of a second too much. Colby landed a glancing blow to his shin. It wasn't a hard one—most of the force was dissipated by his backward motion—but through luck or good management on Colby's part, it landed squarely atop the bruise she had bestowed on him twenty-four hours earlier.

It was, perhaps, undignified for a six-foot-two man to yelp in agony, but that's just what Jase did. He bent over and clutched his wounded shin, rubbing it until the first stinging pain subsided into a dull throb. Colby didn't follow up her advantage by throwing anything at him, even though there was a temptingly large dictionary very close to her hand.

She stood her ground, fists planted on her hips, and

watched him. When he straightened back up, she snarled, "Touch me and I'll give you another set of teeth marks to match the ones you already have." He didn't move toward her so she continued heatedly. "The rules I play by, Jase Culhane, don't include seduction to gain information. Remember that ground rule. It might save your shins."

Her slow smile was pure nasty. "And out of the goodness of my heart I'll tell you something you seem eager to know. Matt plays by my rules, Jase. Everything Matt gets from me, I give him freely. He doesn't have to use your kind of tactics. He doesn't have to!" she finished with hissing fervor.

If Colby thought she'd seen Jase Culhane in a temper, she swiftly realized that what had gone before could have qualified as a mild snit. The mere mention of Matt's name seemed to have the power to enrage him beyond normal bounds. His face became a dark red and then paled abnormally, leaving him sallow beneath his deep tan. *Holy cow!* she thought in the vernacular of her childhood.

Retreat and fight another day, Colby, her mind shrieked. Jase took a step toward her and Colby spun and ran like a startled doe. She was out the library door and halfway down the hall toward the living room and Margy's safe presence before he had time to take another step. He let her go. He never wanted to come that close to rape again.

Colby might not be aware of it, though he rather thought she was from the speed of her exit, but had he laid hands on her, he would have done his best to wipe Matt's imprint from her mind and body, replacing it with his own.

Jase raised a shaking hand to his forehead. He must be going insane, and not slowly insane at that. Angry or not, there was no excuse for his behavior. A seventeen-year-old schoolgirl, for God's sake! Unwilling and deliberately provocative, but still a guest in his home. He went to his study and relocked the door behind him. The next sound heard was the chattering clink of glass on glass. Jase didn't come back out.

Colby catapulted into the living room as though all the furies pursued her. Margy glanced up, then looked more sharply at Colby. Colby's color was hectic and her breathing heavy, and she glanced behind her in some trepidation.

"You and Jase had another set-to?" Margy asked in resignation, lowering the novel she had been reading, though keeping her place with a finger between the pages.

"I think you could safely call it that," Colby responded rather breathlessly, her ear still cocked for Jase's return to the living room.

"Did you throw anything at him?" Margy asked in a tone of academic interest. "I mean, am I going to have to mop up blood or stitch him up?"

Colby grinned slightly, but she was still rather shaken. "No, I didn't heave anything at him, but he could probably use an ice pack for his shin. I kicked him again and I rather think I managed to land on the same spot I did last time."

"Last time?" Margy said faintly. "What last time? Did you all have another fight when you were out riding? I thought I'd managed to referee all the other ones you two have had since you came."

"I kicked him last night while he was abducting me. Bit him too," Colby added with some reminiscent satisfaction. "While he was spanking me. I imagine he still has the marks in his thigh," she concluded with relish.

"Kicked Jase? Bit him in the thigh?" Margy could only repeat Colby's words in a dazed echo. "He spanked you?"

"That was after I swung on him and kicked him. He blocked my punch, which is probably just as well. I might have broken my hand if I'd hit him in the jaw. I think Jase has a very hard head." She rubbed her buttocks reminiscently. "He has a hard hand too."

Margy couldn't help it. It was just too ludicrous. She laughed until tears streamed down her cheeks. Her book fell forgotten to the floor. After all, no book could compete with the real-life drama going on before her eyes. She mopped at her streaming eyes with the back of her hand.

Colby watched her with resigned wryness. "Well, yes, it does sound a bit much when put into words, doesn't it? But I was fighting mad at the time and I do," she admitted modestly, "have a wee bit of a temper."

"And Jase manages to bring it out in full force," choked Margy, going off into another peal of helpless laughter.

"Jase Culhane is the most overbearing, pigheaded, arrogant man I've ever met, surpassing even my father in the wrongheaded belief that he has the right to decide how I'm to live my life." Colby warmed to her theme. "How dare he kidnap a perfect stranger! How dare he set himself up as moral arbiter and judge of my behavior! It's none of his damn business if I want to make my living singing at a nightclub. It's not even my father's business, and Jase is a long way from being my father. He's not my brother or my keeper either," Colby raged on, getting more incensed by the minute, the longer she thought about it.

Margy muttered, "I'm pretty sure Jase has no desire to be either your father or your brother." But Colby didn't hear her, nor would she have heeded the words had she been listening.

She was consumed by her sense of grievance. "I'm twenty-one . . . I'm an adult and fully capable of ordering

106

my own life. Just because I had the good taste to refuse to marry Barry Delaroy and cement the grand and glorious merger between Duncan Associates and Delaroy Plastics—and that's another thing! I will not be included as some sort of a package sweetener for a business deal. If my father thinks that by ruining my job at the club I'll be more amenable to marrying one of his Prince Charmings, has he got another think coming! I'll burn the ears off of his head next time I see him." Colby was pacing furiously up and down the length of the living room now, the possibility of Jase's appearance forgotten.

Margy watched silently, an occasional twitch pulling at her lips. She wasn't sure she understood even a quarter of this, but she stored it all away for later consideration. It would do Colby good to spout off like this. She'd really had an eventful twenty-four hours, and since she was of a volatile temperament and decidedly willful to boot, this whole business was bound to go sorely against her grain. Evidently Jase's behavior (and wasn't *that* the strangest thing!) was just the final straw in this running feud Colby seemed to have going with her father.

She didn't envy Colby's father the next time Colby confronted him. Margy could well imagine that Colby was capable of burning his ears off. She'd already had a limited sample of Colby's capabilities in biting repartee from observing her clashes with Jase. She shuddered to think what would happen if Colby threw aside all restraint. A tongue like a buzz saw.

Colby gradually calmed down. She didn't usually blow up in this manner, but the encounter with Jase had shaken her severely. It had been stupid and dangerous to taunt Jase that way, but the violence of his reaction had appalled her. It had almost been as though the mention of Matt's name put him in a jealous rage, which was ridiculous. He was just a man who couldn't stand being thwarted, and when she'd seen through the purpose of his lovemaking, it infuriated him.

Yes, that was it, she decided in relief. Jase had just wanted to find out who Matt was and what power he might have to effect Colby's rescue. She smiled to herself. And well he might worry about that. If he knew Matt was a policeman, wouldn't that make Mr. Jase Culhane shake in his size-eleven boots? Jase and her father didn't have a legal leg to stand on in this abduction and the knowledge that the police were already involved and were probably searching for her would be an unpleasant shock for Mr. Jase Culhane.

How she'd love to be able to tell Jase just what he'd got himself mixed up in. She sighed regretfully. What a shame she couldn't do it. Not only her safety, but the safety of other people depended on as few people as possible knowing of the police interest and investigation of the club. Matt might be handicapped by her disappearance, but since he now knew that her father was responsible for her disappearance and that basically she was not in any danger—of course he didn't know Jase—the painstaking investigation would go on.

She didn't know whether she'd been able to give Matt enough information to go on for him to effect a speedy rescue. Jase would have had to file a flight plan, but under what name? And it was a very busy airport. Many light aircraft would have taken off that day and it would take time to sift through and trace all the leads.

She'd just have to depend on the assumption that she had to get herself out of this. Perhaps if she got back soon enough, she could repair the damage done by her father's machinations. The club owners wouldn't be at all eager to give her her job back. She was useful to them, but with a man as powerful as Steven Duncan willing to go to such lengths to keep her from working at the club, they would drop her like a hot brick. They didn't need her drawing power that much.

Unless, of course, she could use counterblackmail, threaten to brew up a scandal unless they took her back. It just might work. She'd have to stress the get-back-at-Daddy angle pretty heavily, which wouldn't be hard to do at all, and if she could convince them that she was willing to pull the club into the scandal and all the attendant publicity unless they gave her the job back . . .

Colby grinned to herself. Matt would be livid. He knew as well as she did that one just didn't go about threatening with impunity the kind of people they were dealing with, but it might be worth it to maintain her connection at the club. Matt would have to admit that she had been able to funnel very valuable information to him because of her job. He had told her so several times, and Lt. Matt MacGuire didn't say things like that lightly.

Margy had been watching Colby with some perplexity. First she had paced angrily, letting her frustration and anger vent away in words. But then she had dropped into an armchair, and steepling her fingers, tapping them occasionally against her chin and mouth, she had fallen into a blue reverie. She had looked alternately worried, thoughtful, worried, and then determined.

Margy didn't think, somehow, that Colby was thinking about Jase. There was a stern maturity about her face, and an air of resolution that made Margy shiver slightly. It was almost as though Colby had decided on a course she knew was dangerous but necessary. Suddenly Margy agreed with Jase. It was important to keep Colby at the ranch, and from a passive spectator, she suddenly became an active warden. She'd have to tell Jase, but do it without alerting Colby.

Colby gave her her chance a short while later. Unaware of Margy's sudden shift in status from passive to active participant, Colby smiled agreeably at the older woman and yawned.

"I think I'll go on up, Margy. Last night was rigorous and today has been exhausting, one way and another. I don't imagine tomorrow is going to be any different, unless of course," she concluded hopefully, "Jase suddenly changes his mind and lets me go."

Margy's answering smile merely reinforced the absurdity of that hope. She said, "Sleep well, Colby. Is there anything you need?"

"No, thanks, Margy. Whoever packed me up put in everything but the kitchen sink. I think he must have stripped my apartment bare, except for the plants, and the pots and pans." Colby yawned again and rose to her feet. "See you in the morning, Margy."

Colby had no intention of going to bed, or at least to bed to sleep. She wanted to be safely in her room before Jase made another appearance, and she wanted to be able to move about her room while everyone was downstairs, except for Paul, who was presumably asleep already. She had preparations to make and she'd have to discover where Margy had put the things she was going to need. That might involve a lot of drawer opening and closing, and Colby had a healthy respect for Jase's powers of deduction.

While Colby went her devious way up the stairs, Margy went in search of Jase. It didn't take her too long. He wasn't in the library or the kitchen, and unless he had stormed outside to cool off, that left the study. She knocked softly on the door. An indistinct growl answered her, but the door was locked and the growl hadn't said "Come in." Margy knocked again, more firmly.

"Jase, it's Margy. I have to talk to you. Open the door, please."

She waited patiently until the door lock released and the door swung open. Jase stood in the doorway, barring entrance to his sanctuary, a half-full glass of amber liquid in his hand and a mean expression on his face. "Go away, Margy. If it's about Colby, I don't want to talk about that little witch. Her father should have strangled her at birth."

"And right now you feel as though you'd like to rectify that omission, Jase?" Margy grinned mischievously at him.

"Right now I feel like I want to get drunk, Margy. Are you planning on joining me?" Jase said with sarcastically heavy patience.

My, my, he has got it badly, Margy thought with amusement. She'd never seen Jase in such shape before. "That's what I came to talk to you about," she said with a slight smile. "I do plan to join you."

Jase looked at her in stunned disbelief. He looked down at his half-empty glass and then back up to Margy. Margy was a nondrinker. He'd never even seen her sip a glass of wine. He had the flashing thought that Colby was going to succeed in driving them all 'round the bend.'

Margy put her hand on Jase's hard chest and shoved him backward. For a moment he stood immovable, a granite boulder in her path, but then he gave way, backing up to allow her entrance.

"I didn't want to discuss this with you out in the hall,"

Margy explained. "I didn't want Colby to hear what I have to say to you."

His eyes narrowed. "Read me no lectures, Margy," he warned succinctly.

"I don't intend to, Jase. I just wanted to tell you that I've come around to your way of thinking. I'll help you keep Colby here, for her own good. I'm worried about her if she goes back. There's something strange going on, something that just doesn't add up, and I have a feeling that she's . . . safer . . . here on the ranch, even if you do have the desire to strangle her now and then. I think your control is adequate to cope with even Colby."

"I wish I had as much faith in me as you do," Jase muttered, and downed the rest of the contents of his glass.

"Mmmm. Well, let's just say that I'm sure you won't strangle her," Margy admitted dryly. "I'll be here to see that nothing else happens to her." She gave him a hard look and Jase flushed.

"I do not take advantage of children," he said with dignity.

"I'm sure that there's not a five-year-old living who has anything to fear from you, Jase," Margy said with spurious intent to soothe. "What's that got to do with Colby though? I'd hardly call her a child."

"Just what did Colby tell you?" Jase's face was rapidly assuming the dusky hue of mingled anger and embarrassment.

"About you? Just that she'd kicked you in the shins again. The rest of it was a diatribe against her meddling father. She seems to feel that one of the reasons behind the abduction was her refusal to agree to a marriage he had planned between herself and someone called Barry Delaroy, of Delaroy Plastics, whatever that is. It also seems

112

that he's the latest in a line of prospective husbands her father has presented, for her approval, I mean."

Jase had lost his color again. He made a muffled choking sound and poured himself another drink. "Married? Her father wanted her to get married? The man must be insane. She's nothing but a child, a nasty-tempered spoiled brat who needed more spankings than she ever got!" He tossed down half of his drink in one gulp.

Margy sniggered. "Speaking of spankings, how is your leg? Your thigh, I mean." She began to laugh helplessly again. "Honestly, Jase, your face! I wish you could see your face right now. She's really been giving you fits, hasn't she? I'm sorry, Jase. I won't tease you anymore. You have all you can do to keep up with Colby. I just wanted to let you know that I'll keep a close eye on her here in the house. I assume you'll take care of her outside?"

"Yes," he agreed grimly. "I'll take care of her. Just what did she say about her father's plans to marry her off? Was she engaged to Delaroy?"

"No, I don't think so. She didn't say so. She just said something about refusing to marry him or to ever be a—a package sweetener in one of her father's business deals. Evidently Delaroy wasn't the first candidate Mr. Duncan had presented for the hand of the princess."

Jase ground his teeth audibly. "With a father like that one, no wonder Colby went off the rails. There are words for men like him."

"Well, if there are, I rather imagine Colby has laid tongue to them all. She was most definite in her refusal to go along with his plans, I gather, and said she'd burn his ears off next time she saw him. I imagine that she has enough bones to pick with him by now to assemble a full-size dinosaur." Margy shook her head admiringly. "I've always heard the expression 'I'd love to be a fly on the wall' and never really understood it before, but now I do. What a clash that one is going to be."

"I imagine you're right. I think I begin to see why Davis was ready to back off," he finished almost to himself. "Perhaps he has been 'a fly on the wall' once or twice."

Margy would have liked for Jase to explain Davis but judged that she had done what she came to do and now it was time to depart. Jase had allowed her more license than she had expected, but she wasn't one to push her luck.

"Well, it's been a long day, Jase. I'm away to bed. Er . . . I gather you'll be near the house for the next few days?"

He chuckled ruefully. "Yes, Margy, I'll be around. It's a good thing Jim is a good foreman. He'll have to be for a while. Colby will run rings around anyone else I set to watch her, and besides, it's a job I prefer to do personally." He grinned again, a small boy bent on mischief. "My shins are already well broken in. No sense crippling anyone else."

"Good night, Jase."

"Good night, Margy."

Margy went straight up to bed. Jase would check the house and turn off the rest of the lights before he went up. There was no light showing beneath Colby's door and there was no sound from within. Resting up for the next day's fray, Margy presumed.

CHAPTER FIVE

Colby wasn't asleep. She was in bed, beneath the covers, but her night attire was decidedly odd. She wore a thin navy-blue long-sleeved jersey shirt that was buttoned to the neck and tucked into navy knit warmup pants. She wore dark socks and her hair was pulled back and braided in one long braid. A small handkerchief-wrapped bundle was thrust beneath her pillow and one hand lay protectively curled around it. Her door was locked, and even if Jase tried it on his way to bed, he would probably think it a normal enough precaution, considering the way they had parted such a short while ago.

Colby lay in the dark, staring at a ceiling she could not see, and thought about Jase. There had been violence in his face as they confronted each other in the library. She had run from the slipping control she had read in the step he had taken toward her, but it hadn't been fear of another spanking she had been fleeing.

There had been a primitive, sensual desire in those silvery eyes, a wild hunger that touched a deep chord in the pit of her stomach even as she ran, as a mare might run from a stallion, the last break for freedom before he brought her under his protection. What if she had not run?

If Jase had taken more than the one step, if he had

caught her before she fled the library, would the searing flames that had flickered in his eyes have lit fires in her own, the clear blue flame of the hottest fire? Could he have reined himself to tenderness, gentling her into acceptance of his domination, or would she have fought him wildly, clawing and biting, refusing him any form of submission?

For the first time in her life Colby was unsure of her feelings about a man. She had been contemptuous of the men her father had offered as candidates for her hand and body. Any man who allows a girl's father to buy him as a present for his daughter had three strikes against him as any sort of husband from the start.

Colby stood up to her father. She could have no respect for any man who could not do the same. She had no desire to prop up her husband in a struggle against domination by her father, and Steven Duncan was a dominant and domineering man—whenever he could get away with it, which was most of the time. Any husband he picked for Colby, his only child, would be *his* creature.

For all that Jase had kidnapped her at her father's behest, somehow Colby knew that Jase was no one's man save his own. She didn't know why Jase had agreed to participate, although she planned to find out, but it was not for money, Somehow, instinctively, she knew that. No one could buy this man, and her father was too good a judge of men to have tried.

Jase wanted her. He might not like what he knew of her, obviously he didn't, but desire was not always allied with liking. For that matter, she wasn't sure she liked Jase either, mostly she had this nearly uncontrollable urge to hit him with a blunt instrument. She recognized that this was also unfortunately significant in its own way.

Bland indifference was impregnable. Hate and love were

116

strong emotions and left one vulnerable. Her emotions were too churned for her to be sure just what she really felt about Jase, but it wasn't indifference. That much had been clear to her the first time their eyes had clashed in that little room at the airport. She had been sensitive to the disgust in his eyes as he ran them insultingly up and down her figure—what he could see of it beneath the open raincoat. And that was strange. She had seen disgust, but no surprise. He had expected her to look disreputable. Just what had her father told him?

And that led again to the thought she had briefly considered and then put away for later examination. Just what lay behind this kidnapping? The more she thought about it, the more she was sure it was not motivated by a desire to wreck her singing career at the club. It was too drastic a solution.

Her father had always made sure one of his flunkies attended each of her performances. She had seen and recognized them, looking uncomfortable and button-down, and for devilment she had often flirted mildly with an occasional one as she strolled through the tables during her act. To a man they had always reacted like beached fish, mouths agape and eyes staring from their heads. Worth their jobs to get familiar with the boss's daughter, no matter what her getup!

Had one of them, brighter than most, stumbled onto the hidden purpose of the club? Was her father trying to remove her from a danger he thought she had not sensed? Or, worse and worse, could he have put two and three together properly and understood her hidden purpose? Had he deliberately interfered with Matt's investigation, risking the ruin of all she had labored for these long distasteful months because of concern for her safety?

Her doorknob rattled faintly, chopping off her train of thought. She had been so lost in speculations that she had not heard Jase come up the stairs. She heard the slight scrape as the knob twisted back and forth and found entry denied by lock and key. It was a long moment before the steps she was now listening for moved on down the hall toward Jase's room.

Colby tried to slow her breathing, deliberately taking deep breaths in an effort to pace her suddenly racing heart. Perhaps it was her imagination, but there had been a quality of decision about that long pause outside her door, as if Jase had been debating whether or not to open the door. Irrational fears, she was sure, because the door was locked, but Colby couldn't escape the feeling that had he so decided, Jase would have come into her room, locked door or not.

Just what Jase would have done to her had he indeed come in and found her dressed and with her incriminating little packet clutched in her hand, Colby shuddered to think. Nerves made her throat and mouth dry and she wished she had had the foresight to put a glass of water by her bed. This was worse than the usual attacks of stage fright she was prone to at times. She could only hope that, as when she actually began her performances, the fright would recede and she would be able to concentrate on the job at hand. It wouldn't do at all to have shaky hands for tonight's performance!

Her watch, the luminous dial glowing faintly, told her the house had been quiet for over an hour, with only the occasional creak as timbers shifted to break the palpable silence. If she left it any longer, she might not have the courage to even throw back the covers, she mocked herself. The truth was, she couldn't stand the inactivity any longer. *Ready or not, here I come,* she thought with a silent twist of her lips. She threw back the covers.

On silent and as nearly weightless feet as she could make them, she made her way to her bedroom door, eyes closed to attune her senses to the deep blackness. She had mapped an unobstructed path in her mind and was pleased to find that she had been able to follow it exactly. The doorknob was right where her hand reached for it. She unlocked and turned the knob silently.

Since she was careful, the knob was silent, not like when Jase had rattled it back and forth. The door swung open without a creak, air from the hall lapping against her face and the feeling of space awakening the sensors of her skin. She didn't have the finely attuned sensitivity of a blind person, but she would milk the utmost from her limited capabilities.

She made a sharp right turn out into the hall, facing the stairs. She had already looked to her left; there was no light showing beneath any door, especially Jase's. With the fingers of her right hand ever so lightly touching the wall and her precious package gripped tightly in her left, Colby carefully began to make her way to the head of the stairs. Her eyes were open, straining in the darkness, but they were effectively useless to her in the lightless void.

She was at the top of the stairs. She looked down to where the bottom lay, even though she couldn't see it. There was absolutely no sound except her quiet breathing, which she consciously kept as silent as possible. There was no light either so she cautiously began her descent, counting each step as she took it. She had no desire to jar her spine through her skull by taking a step that wasn't there when she reached the bottom.

As she had hoped, now that she was finally doing something all her nervousness had vanished. She squashed a smug exhilaration firmly—too soon to crow—but her helplessness had galled severely. Her stockinged feet met the final step and she swung her left foot out in an exploratory arc just to make sure that it was indeed the bottom. Caution would cost her nothing.

She glanced at her watch. It had taken her five minutes to negotiate the upper hall and the stairs. Oh, well, she wasn't in a race against the clock. She had all night if need be. When she reached the kitchen, there was moonlight to ease the darkness and she ghosted across the room, a dark shadow with glimmering face and hands floating disembodied because of her dark, carefully chosen clothes. Only the soft rhythmic pad of her stockinged feet as they slipped across the floor gave evidence that she was flesh and blood and not a drifting spirit.

She opened the door to the pantry slowly, but like everything in this house, it was in perfect order and it swung gaping with oiled silence. There was a light she could have switched on after cautiously closing the door, but it would mean destroying her night vision so she found the flashlight she had chosen by feel. With a muffling hand over the lens, she tested it, watching the skin of her hand take on a red glow as the light spent itself into her cupped palm.

Back out of the pantry, through the kitchen, and into the twists and turns that left her before Jase's study door. Just on the off chance, she gently tried the handle. Still locked. She grinned slightly. Perhaps she could do something about that.

She knelt and laid the small package she had carried on the floor by the door. In the shaded light of the flashlight she had now switched on, it looked just like what it was—a gold plastic nail kit. She opened the snap and spread the case and surveyed the implements within with satisfaction. Everything for beautiful nails and cuticles. Her mouth curved delightedly.

Delicately she pressed the hidden pressure points and lifted aside the innocuous orange sticks, nail files, and scissors, still in their places. Beneath them lay the cleverly concealed real purpose of this kit. Winking back up at her in the flashlight's glow were the slender steel burglar's delight—a complete set of picklocks. Matt had ceremoniously presented the kit to her, fresh from the police department that specialized in devising such necessary goodies, as soon as her instructor told him she had completed the lockpicking course.

Matt had also given her a lecture about not trying any grandstand plays such as breaking into the manager's room and locked desk drawers or filing cabinets, at least not without his express permission. He had emphasized that the course and the implements were merely in the nature of insurance against some unlikely contingency.

She had never carried the kit with her to the club, but had kept it among her other toiletries. Whoever had packed for her had included it and for his thoroughness, if nothing else, she blessed him. It might, in some small measure, mitigate the general curse she had called down on everyone concerned with this mess.

She examined the lock carefully, the calm voice of her instructor echoing in her brain as he had lectured her on types and constructions of locks. Should be a straightforward job, she decided in relief. The lock wasn't really meant for security, just privacy.

Taking a deep breath and releasing it slowly with a small hiss, she chose one of the slender instruments and set to work. It took ninety seconds before the slight click announced success. Not bad. She had done better, but she wasn't one to quibble with success. She pushed the door open slightly and then tidily replaced the pick and the concealing layer over them. If she were caught going back to bed she might find it embarrassing to explain why she was carrying around a nail kit in her nocturnal perambulations, but it would be nothing to trying to explain the set of picklocks.

Besides, with luck Jase wouldn't realize that the sanctity of his study had been breached until it was too late. By then, hopefully, she'd be long gone. The thought gave her a curious qualm, which she quickly brushed away. She already knew the repercussions from this whole mess were going to be far-reaching and it would be a long time before she recovered, if ever.

She rose to her feet and went into the study, noiselessly closing and locking the door behind her. Once inside, she swept her light over the room in a flickering survey. It was a large room, on a scale with all the other rooms of this house, high ceilinged and gracious.

The diffuse circle of light with its brighter center circle touched here and there on various objects. A wall map, two tall bookcases, filing cabinets, a comfortable-looking couch with cushions plumped invitingly at one end, just right for a catnap, and everywhere the rich somber glow of darkly polished paneling. A desk faced outward into the room. The high-backed chair that normally sat behind it was shoved away and positioned so that whoever sat in it last had had a clear view out of the now closed windows. Perhaps Jase had sat there, his feet propped on the window ledge, and stared out the window, devising more schemes to thwart her desire to escape. She snorted softly at her own fancies.

She directed her light back at the desk. Books, weighty reference tomes, were piled to one side, little bits of torn-paper markers jutting from between the pages. A typewriter, a sheet of paper curling in its roller, flanked the books, along with several sheets of typescript. And there, unnoticed before, a phone!

Colby could have done a jig in ecstasy. There had been phone jacks in other rooms, her own bedroom among them, but no sign of a phone. Margy had admitted that they had phone communication but would say no more.

Colby reached out an eager hand for the receiver. Matt could have the call traced or perhaps the number would be on the phone itself. It would be a simple matter for him to get the location of the phone from the phone company if she could tell him the number, or there'd be business letters with addresses on them. Just give her a few minutes among the files and . . .

She pressed the receiver to her ear and reached to dial the familiar number. Let Jase pay for the phone call. Serve him right. Her hand froze even as her finger slotted into the hole for the first number. The phone was dead. There was no familiar dial tone buzzing in her ear. Colby muttered softly in disgust. She jiggled the cut-off buttons experimentally. Nothing.

In a last ditch hope she began to follow the cord as it looped down over the desk and ran toward the wall. Perhaps the jack had pulled loose, or maybe Jase had deliberately unplugged it. There was tension in the cord so it was still attached to something, but perhaps the connection was imperfect. Her light trailed along the length of the cord until it came to . . . a hand! A very large tanned hand with long sinewy fingers that she recognized with a shrinking heart.

The disembodied hand began to twirl the end of the cord and the jack attached to it in maddeningly casual circles. There was a creak as the high-backed chair began to revolve and the hand turned out of the circle of light as jean-clad legs moved into it. The flashlight tilted automatically, traveling up the seated figure, the light touching on the partially unbuttoned checked shirt and reaching the deeply tanned neck and angle of the chin before the hand that had held the phone cord came up to stop its progress. Automatically she noted the soft thump of the jack as it fell to the floor beside the chair.

"No flashlight in my eyes, please, Colby," came the familiar drawling tones. "I think it's time for a brighter light, don't you? I wouldn't want you to bruise your shins in an unfamiliar dark room."

Jase rose from the chair. She could feel him looming over her in the darkness. She might have bolted, but his hand was firm and warning around her wrist. The clasp was gentle now, but she knew if she tried to jerk away it would clamp tightly like a steel manacle.

He took a step beside her and brushed against her as he leaned over the desk, fumbling slightly before light flooded forth, bright at first to her dark-accustomed eyes, then resolving itself into light from a reading lamp, making a warm pool on the desk. Jase took the flashlight from her unresisting hand and switched it off before he tossed it on the desk, where it rocked back and forth slightly from the force of the ungentle thump. It was the only betrayal of the anger he must be damping down, because when Colby met his eyes, she could see only amusement and mockery glinting in those silver depths.

"I've got to hand it to you, honey. You're a trier. What

magic did you use to walk through that locked door, hmmm?"

Colby glared at him silently. Jase's eye was caught by the gleam of the little gold case on his desk where she had dropped it while she used the phone, or tried to. He didn't release her wrist, picking up the little case with his free hand. He hefted it speculatively before he snapped the latch back with his thumb.

His eyebrows rose in comical astonishment as he surveyed the innocuous nail kit. Colby hid a smirk, wisely as it turned out. He looked at her closely and said, "I know women can do a lot of things with a hairpin, but this is the first time I've ever heard of one who could pick a lock with an orange stick."

Colby ostentatiously inspected her nails on her free hand and said, "A girl likes to make the most of her hands. My mother always says well-kept nails are a sign of good grooming." She tugged slightly at her imprisoned wrist but desisted when Jase's fingers tightened warningly. "You must have left your door unlocked by mistake." She smiled innocently up at him.

"How careless of me," Jase responded dryly. "All these gadgets you women use fascinate me," he continued smoothly as he began to poke and prod at the case.

Colby watched in resignation until he finally hit the pressure point and the false base of the little case loosened. Jase lifted the top layer away and laid it on the desk. He whistled softly at the variety of implements lying revealed in the case now and looked up to scan her slightly flushed face.

"What an interesting little case this is, Grandma. Did you get it with Green Stamps? Not your issue nail kit, I would imagine. What handy little department store did you find this at, I wonder?" He shook her imprisoned wrist slightly in emphasis.

Colby firmed her lips mutinously and refused to answer, but she didn't really believe Jase was going to let her get away with pleading the Fifth. He might be speaking softly and calmly, with faintly humorous undertones, but there was a simmering tension growing between them that prickled the back of her neck. He wanted answers and he meant to get them.

"Where did you get this, Colby? And more importantly, who taught you how to use it? I don't imagine there are many girls your age who have the various accomplishments you seem to have, and I'd give a lot to know why you've felt it necessary to develop so many of them." Jase's voice was soft and coaxing, much like the one he had used on her in the library. Colby wasn't going to be so easily won over this time. No one had ever accused her of being a slow learner.

"I took Lockpicking One and Two in school," she responded flippantly. "It was an elective and appealed to me more than Basket Weaving Three and Four. I mean, after all, when you've woven one basket, you've woven them all."

"Ask a silly question . . ." Jase muttered. He carefully put the case back together and shut it. He let go of Colby's wrist but at the same time said softly, "Don't go away, Colby," while he bent to put the case in a drawer of the desk. He then pulled a small key from his pocket and locked the drawer, slipping the key back into his jeans pocket.

"Did you also take Pickpocket One and Two, my little delinquent? I guess I'll have to keep your hands occupied with other things." He put his hands on her shoulders and

126

turned her away from the desk and directed her toward the couch.

Colby looked longingly at the study door, but as if he could read her thoughts, Jase's hands flexed on her shoulders as a tiger flexes his paws before he extends his claws. He leaned forward and his words whispered past her ear. "I'd catch you before you got two steps, Colby kitten. Go curl up on the couch like a good little girl. I'm going to stroke your fur a bit and we'll see if you know how to purr as well as bite and scratch!"

"Cats are easy to rub the wrong way, Jase," she warned him pertly, but her voice sounded strangely hollow even to herself. Jase's words were teasing, taken at surface value, but as she threw a swift glance at him back over her shoulder, his chin and mouth had a stern set she disliked exceedingly.

She walked to the couch but didn't sit as directed. She was now desperately regretting her foray into breaking and entering, not that she would have regretted it had it come off—but who would have expected that Jase would be lying in wait for her to try just what she had?

She tried for a reasonable tone. "Jase, you caught me red-handed. I admit it, but I gave no parole, you know."

He was standing so close behind her that the heat from his body reached out to her in a tangible wave. "Does that mean you're offering parole now?" he asked softly in her ear. His hands were light on her shoulders and the thumbs were slowly massaging the tense muscles in the nape of her neck.

"No." The word was not emphatic, more regretful, but none the less definite for that. "I can't, Jase. I must go back, and as soon as possible. If you won't let me go, I must find a way myself."

127

He spun her around and tilted her chin up so she met his eyes. "Why, Colby? Why is it so important that you go back? Do those people mean so much to you that you strain every nerve and sinew to get back to them?"

Gently but firmly he forced her to subside onto the couch. He sat down beside her and captured her hands in one of his big ones. With the other hand he pulled her plait around and released it, combing through the strands with his fingers until her hair was free around her shoulders. That done, he once again captured her chin and said insistently, "Why, Colby? Help me to understand."

"My job is important to me, Jase. I signed a contract. I must honor it, in spite of my father. He has no right to force me to breach it. People are depending on me."

Jase's face was a study in bewilderment. "What job? What contract?"

"My contract with the club as a singer," she explained patiently. "Why do you think I was dressed in that outlandish getup when Davis lured me to the airport? I was on my way to the club for the evening's performance and I was running late so I changed at my apartment. I usually wait until I get to the club to do the makeup and costume, but I knew I wasn't going to have time so—"

She broke off and looked closely at Jase. She could see he hadn't understood a word she was saying. "Good heavens, man, you don't think I go around dressed like a tramp all the time, do you?"

A hot tide of color flooded his face. Colby's eyes narrowed dangerously and her chin took on a fighting jut. Now she was the interrogator, and her voice dropped to a silken purr. She pulled her hands from Jase's relaxed clasp and moved back away from him on the couch so that there was no physical contact between them at all. "Just what did my darling daddy tell you about me, Jase? Just what do you think I am?"

Jase answered her question with a question. "How old are you, Colby?"

She looked at him askance. What had her age to do with anything? But she answered him nonetheless. It seemed important to him. "I'm twenty-one. I was twenty-one several months ago."

She didn't understand his expression. Relief and disgust seemed mingled in equal parts. However, she did catch the gist of his wryly muttered comment, "At least I won't be cradle robbing."

Her cheeks pinked, and the look in his eyes as they looked over her body made them flame even more hectically. It was becoming unpleasantly clear that Daddy had been playing ducks and drakes with the truth on a rather grandiose scale. She looked at Jase inquiringly.

"Well, to begin with, your father told me you were only seventeen, thus underage and, therefore, your precipitate visit to the ranch was a visit, not a technical abduction. I wouldn't have agreed to be a party to it in the first place if I'd known your true age."

Colby was admiringly astounded at her father's willingness to take chances and twist the truth like a pretzel. "But when you saw me for the first time, couldn't you tell I wasn't any seventeen-year-old schoolgirl?" she asked incredulously.

"Honey, when I first saw you, you could have been thirty for all I knew, but from what else your father told me, I wasn't surprised that you didn't look seventeen. I'd have been surprised if you had!"

"Umm. I didn't like the first part, but I have a feeling

that I'm going to like what comes next even less. Just what else did he tell you?" Colby's hands clenched in her lap.

Jase seemed really embarrassed now. "Well, you won't like it," he admitted with chagrin. "I don't like it myself, now more than ever. He said you spent a lot of time at a rather unsavory nightclub, associating with a very wild bunch of people. He hinted at drug involvement and a . . . er . . . rather promiscuous life-style. He said that because of a trust established on your grandmother's death, you had your own money and that he and your mother had been unable to stop you from moving into your own apartment, short of making you a ward of the court, which he was loath to do."

Colby's face had gone icily blank at the mention of drugs. When Jase went on to describe her father's hints about her morals, she ground her teeth together so hard, her jaw was sore. How dare he! She'd never speak to her father again, after, of course, she gave herself the pleasure of telling him exactly what she thought of *his* manners and morals.

"Colby, why would your father go to such lengths? He must have known he couldn't get away with it for long. Just what did he hope to accomplish?" Jase was puzzled. There still was too much that didn't add up. Steven Duncan would have to have most pressing reasons to go to such lengths.

"He didn't like me working at that club," Colby said absently. She was still examining the possibility that her father had somehow stumbled onto her undercover work for Matt. It was the only thing that would adequately explain all the urgency of her abduction. Somehow her father knew! And he must have known that things were coming to a head because he couldn't hope to hold her

130

incommunicado for more than a short while, and he knew her well enough to know that she would do her best to reinstate herself at the club.

That conclusion opened up several more disquieting possibilities. Had the security of Matt's department and investigation been breached? Colby knew her father had many lines of information. Did one of them reach into the police department? Or had he got hints from the men he had set to watch her and deduced the rest, knowing of her involvement through Sandi's death?

"Why didn't he want you working at the club, Colby?" Getting information from this girl was harder than pulling chickens' teeth, Jase thought. "Was it such a bad place?"

"Oh, not too bad as such places go," Colby determinedly understated. "I think it really galled him that I wouldn't let him buy a record company or at least part of one, or use his influence to launch a glossy singing career for his child. My father likes to be in control of things, you know," she observed with some bitterness. "He also had other plans I didn't feel inclined to go along with."

"You mean Barry Delaroy?" Jase asked tightly.

"How'd you know about that?" Colby asked with some surprise. "I hardly think my father would tell anyone about it. We had one of our more notable rows about that little scheme of his and he didn't like losing. A son-in-law is easier to manipulate than a business competitor. My father likes to use finesse when he can, but he's not averse to the bludgeon when all else fails."

"You said something about it to Margy, or if not to Margy, to yourself out loud right after our confrontation in the library. She mentioned it to me; she thought I might be interested." Jase considered this a masterly understatement. "I rather gathered Delaroy was not the first suitor to your hand?"

"No," Colby admitted brusquely. "My father feels if you have a negotiable asset like a marriageable daughter you might as well use her. He and my mother are happy enough, but it wasn't a love match for either of them. My father sees no reason why some similar arrangement wouldn't work equally well for me, especially if it increased the holdings of Duncan Associates, which he is at some pains to remind me will be all mine someday. As if I care!" Colby fairly snorted. "Duncan Associates may be the be-all and end-all for my father, but I think it's nothing less than a millstone, and I have no desire to have it draped around *my* neck!"

"Hmmm. I don't imagine that's a very popular opinion with your father." Jase smiled.

"Heresy, rank heresy." Colby grinned back. "And what really frosted him was when he twitted me about being able to boast of my independence of Duncan Associates' bounty because I had my grandmother's trust income. I fixed him. I didn't cash the quarterly checks and lived off my salary from the club, and very comfortably, I might add."

"I can almost pity your father," Jase said softly. "I had some very hard thoughts about him, you know, when Margy told me about Delaroy and the others, and I still thought you were only seventeen. Not that I like it any better now that I know you're of age," he added hastily. "I imagine it must really gall him to lose a round to a chit of a girl, even his own daughter."

Colby chuckled. "Well, he's rather torn. He likes to win, but he has a sneaking respect for me and the fact that I stand up to him successfully. Like most strong men, he respects strength, even in opposition to him, and since I'm his daughter, it tickles some paternal nerve to think of me as a chip off the old granite. The rub comes because we don't have the same ideas about what's really important in life. Our priorities are different."

There was a cozy intimacy developing between the two people on the couch. The lateness of the hour, the shaded light of the desk lamp, and the silence of the house around them kept their voices hushed. Colby had relaxed almost insensibly, the tensions arising from her abduction flowing away. Jase knew most of the story now, knew of her father's duplicity, and he wouldn't keep her. Tomorrow she'd be on her way back and perhaps she and Matt could still salvage something.

She sighed and stretched, stifling a half yawn. Lord, she was tired. Jase cautiously moved nearer and laid a supportive arm around her shoulders, drawing her gently over to lean against him. His hold was warm and protective and she subsided against his chest, tucked into the clasp of his arms with a small murmur of content. It was so nice not to be on the defensive with him. She made a little instinctive, nestling movement and felt Jase's cheek come down to lie atop her head.

They sat like that for a while, drowsily content to be in harmony at last, and when Jase's hand began to stroke softly up and down her shoulder and arm, Colby merely nestled closer to him. When he tilted her chin up for a gentle kiss, it was surely a logical extension of the warm comfort they were both enjoying. She gladly met him halfway.

Bonfires from little sparks grow, and Colby and Jase lit a conflagration. It would always be thus with them. Fighting or loving, there seemed to be no room for half measures between them. The first tentative, gentle kisses deepened swiftly, and Colby's arms went up to clasp around Jase's neck. This was magic! Her mouth opened beneath the questing touch of his and she felt rather than heard the wordless murmur of desire in his throat.

It was indeed a comfortable couch, she thought dazedly. Somehow, unnoticed, she and Jase had stretched out full length on the couch together and she felt the exciting imprint of his long hard body along every inch of hers. He was so warm and vital and she had never experienced such an intimate embrace from a man before. Colby pulled herself closer to him. The couch back was behind her and Jase was beside her; she curled her stockinged toes in sensual content.

"Purr, little kitten," Jase whispered with the faintest ghost of delighted amusement, and an answering smile lifted her lips. They had wasted so much time in snarling and snapping, Colby thought incoherently. This was so much nicer!

"Oh, Colby, you drive a man mad, you do," Jase groaned, rapidly losing what small remnants of control still remained to him. He buried his face in her throat and began to lay a hot track of kisses, each kiss marking another button undone.

Colby was busy running her fingers through the short inky silk of his hair, flexing her fingertips in his scalp as a kitten might knead with sheathed claws. She ran the fingers of one hand down the back of his muscular neck, delighting in the prickly rasp of the short hairs on his nape. Her hand delved beneath the collar of his shirt, spreading over the flexing muscles of his back, tracing the line of his spine as far as she could reach, until his shirt hindered her.

Suddenly she wanted to feel the warmth of his bare skin against her own. She was hazily aware that Jase had managed to undo all of the buttons on her own shirt while she had been otherwise occupied, and it seemed only fair that his own suffer the same fate. She planted one small hand in the middle of his chest and shoved upward.

He resisted momentarily, being otherwise occupied with the curving swell of the side of her breast, but her persistence finally caught his attention and he lifted his head. It took a moment for his slightly glazed eyes to focus and another moment to enable muscles previously used for kissing to reshape themselves for a husky whisper.

"What's wrong, sweetheart? Am I too heavy on you?" he asked huskily.

Her smile caused the breath to catch in his throat, and she didn't answer him in words. Her free hand came up and began to work at the buttons of his shirt, dexterously slipping them from the buttonholes, which were all too ready to release them anyway. The blaze in Jase's silvery eyes could have glowed in the dark. He lifted and shifted slightly to facilitate her task, and with one hand pulled his shirt free of his jeans after she had done with the buttons.

Jase was leaning on one elbow, one leg pinning the lower half of Colby's body to the couch, but it wasn't to keep her from escaping, because struggle was the farthest thing from her mind. Jase affected her like a potent wine and her only thought was to drain the draft he offered her to the sweet dregs.

When his own shirt hung open, he used his free hand to spread Colby's and she in turn lifted her hips slightly to facilitate his desire to pull it free of the waistband of her warmup pants. Since she hadn't bothered with a bra, something Jase had been aware of since he first snapped on the desk light, there was no further barrier to his eyes and gentle hands. With a slightly shaky fingertip he traced a line from the hollow of her throat, down between her breasts. His hand encompassed the firm fullness as though sized exactly for it, and he drew in his breath sharply as he felt the nipple thrust warmly into the hollow of his palm.

"Colby darling," he groaned softly. "You're so beautiful." He bent his head to taste his way up the curving slope of the breast he had been fondling, moving his hand down to cup the side with inward curving finger and thumb, his other fingers spreading over the silky warm skin of her side. At the warm, drawing pressure from his lips Colby couldn't suppress a small whimpering moan and an involuntary arch of her back. She wanted to be closer to him, to move right up into his body. Her fingers kneaded and pressed into the hard muscles of his back.

The thumb of his free hand was busy, gently rubbing against the erect nipple of her other breast. Each backward and forward stroke set off sharp darts of pleasurable sensation that enhanced the sensual excitement he was building in her body, as his mouth luxuriated in the taste and texture of her breast. His tongue traced gentle circles around the darkened aureole and teased the hard nipple. He nursed as a baby might, but drew pleasure, not milk, into the hot avidity of his mouth.

Colby felt a rush of burning, melting passion arc through her body, encompassing every fiber of her flesh, but localizing in the pleasure points of her breasts and flowering deep in the center of her loins. Her eyes were closed, the better to assimilate all the marvelous, totally new sensations that were flooding through her whole being. No man had ever touched her, ever seen her, as Jase touched and saw her, and suddenly she knew that even the thought of another man was intolerable, never to be considered. Jase was her man, and she pulled herself to him in an ecstasy of possession and surrender.

Jase was kissing the angle of her neck and shoulder at the time and the sudden thrust of her warm breasts against his bare chest snapped what modicum of control he had managed to retain, little enough though that had been. He lifted his head and muttered, "Oh, Colby honey. I don't want to wait until we're married. I want you now. Say you want me. We'll go into town tomorrow and see about a license, but . . ." The rest of his words were muffled as he buried his face in her neck.

Colby had answered him in kind, whispering, "Oh, Jase, I love you. I want you too, darling," before the last part of his sentence made connections in her rather fevered brain. The storm of emotion she was experiencing was not at all conducive to rational thought or conversation.

Suddenly, however, the meaning of his words crashed through the sensual haze she was floating in. Tomorrow . . . tomorrow she had to return. She had to try to salvage what she could of Matt's investigation! She wanted to marry Jase—oh, how she wanted it—but she had to finish her job first.

Jase felt her stiffen and misinterpreted her reaction. His hands played soothing magic over her skin, gentling her, he thought, out of virginal fears. He murmured reassuring words, "Easy, honey. I'll be gentle. I love you, Colby kitten. I won't hurt you, darling."

He put his hand at her waist, starting to ease her warm-ups down. Colby laid a detaining hand over his, exerting no pressure, but not needing to. Jase loved her. He would not force her beyond mutual desiring, and he moved his hand back up to rest just below her breast.

"What is it, love? Tell me, Colby. Do you want to wait until we're married?" It was strange, he thought, they knew so little and yet so much about each other. It would be hard, for she burned in his blood, but he could rein himself to wait if that was what she wanted. He wanted no regrets for her, even if it meant that he had to live beneath a cold shower until he could slide the ring on her finger.

Colby laid a loving hand along his cheek, reveling in the concern that softened the hard planes of his face. He loved her; he would understand. "It's not that, Jase. I want you now too. It's just that we can't get married right away. In a few weeks, I promise, but I have to go back first. I'll come back as soon as I can, but I must go."

She began to lay tasting kisses on his chest, nuzzling into the curling cloud of hairs that furred it, touching her tongue to the slightly salty skin beneath. She missed, therefore, the puzzled frown and then the grim drawing together of his eyebrows. He caught her chin in his hand, tilting her face up so that he could see her eyes, which were drooping closed again as the sensual languor stole back over her. She wiggled slightly against him in innocent allurement and he caught his breath sharply.

"Colby, stop that!" he ordered her sternly. Her eyes flew wide open and she looped her arm around his neck, seeking to pull him back down to her.

"Kiss me, Jase. Make love to me, darling. I want you now," she murmured provocatively. She had never seduced a man before, but it couldn't be all that difficult. Women managed to accomplish it every day and she was pretty sure she had all the right instincts, especially where Jase was concerned.

"Colby!" There was unmistakable warning in that one word. She stopped wiggling and watched him warily.

"What, darling?" she questioned him with dulcet submissiveness.

His voice was calm, but she knew that tone. "Why can't we get married right away? You're not going back to the club, you know. My wife doesn't need to work to prove her independence. Independence is a state of mind, not a bank balance. I'm not your father, Colby. I'm going to be your husband and your lover, in whichever order you choose."

"I choose lover now." She smiled up at him.

"And husband when?" he persisted.

Why did she have to fall in love with such a stubborn man? Seduction was harder than it looked. She just needed more practice, she supposed.

"Can't we talk about that later, darling?"

He sat up abruptly and buttoned up her shirt, putting temptation if not behind him at least out of sight for a while. Colby lay on the couch for a little while longer, but when Jase began to button up his own shirt, she knew it was useless. She sat up with a small groan and swung her legs over the edge of the couch, leaning back to contemplate some distant point on the far wall.

Jase was right. He wasn't her father, but he showed all the same uncomfortable tendencies to demand explanations and wherefores as her father had when she first began to work at the club. She wouldn't lie to Jase, even by omission, as she had to her father, but she had hoped to be able to avoid full disclosure of all the reasons behind the necessity of her return. She should have known better.

139

Once she admitted that she loved him and would marry him, he wouldn't be a laggard lover. Her mouth curved in a smile at the thought of Jase as a lover.

She looked at him, the trend of her thoughts showing clearly in the quality of her smile and the loving look she gave him. "If you were a book, Colby, you'd be banned in Boston," he informed her dryly. "Don't look at me that way. You make me nervous. And don't ask me, 'Look at you how, Jase?' because you damn well know what I'm talking about. Don't think you can distract me indefinitely with your incredibly sexy body and avoid answering my questions. I may be crazy about you, but I'm not so crazy that I can't tell when you're trying to pull the wool over my eyes." He fixed her with a piercing stare. "I'll ask you again, Colby. Why can't we get married right away, as soon as we get the license, in fact?"

"You won't take my word that I have to finish up my contract at the club?" she asked hopefully.

"No."

"I didn't think you would," she said regretfully. She bowed to the inevitable. She wasn't worried about breaching security in telling Jase about Matt's investigation, because she knew Jase could be trusted implicitly. He just wasn't going to be happy to hear of her involvement, even with impeccably worthy motives, in a police investigation of a narcotics ring. It was going to take tact, diplomacy, and soothing words. She'd have to present it to him carefully.

CHAPTER SIX

"The club is a narcotics drop. I'm working as an under-cover agent in conjunction with the police narcotics squad and a federal task force. Word has come down that some-thing big is on, and Matt thinks that we can close down the whole operation by the end of the month if I can find out when the new shipment is due in. That's why I have to go back, and as soon as possible."

"Who the hell is Matt?" Jase thundered.

"Matt?" Colby squeaked. Whatever reaction she had expected, it hadn't been that one.

"Yes, Matt. I'm sick to death of that name. It seems to crop up far too often for my peace of mind and I want to know who he is," Jase growled.

"M-Matt is Lieutenant Matthew MacGuire, head of the narcotics division and my unofficial boss. I'm not actually a member of the force, you see, just sort of a . . . um . . . civilian ally."

She watched him from the corner of her eye. Jase was scowling blackly and Colby decided to let him ask the questions. No sense in telling him more than he wanted to know. He really was jealous of Matt. Maybe he'd be con-tent to concentrate on him and skim over the rest. *Ha, fat chance, Colby,* that inner voice jeered. For once she was afraid the inner voice knew whereof it spoke.

"Just how closely do you work with Lieutenant Mac-Guire?" Jase asked.

"Matt MacGuire is fifty-four years old, has a beer belly, a darling wife named Peg, and two children, one of whom has recently presented him with twin girls for his first grandchildren," she enumerated resignedly, answering the spirit rather than the specific words of his question.

"Oh."

"Yes, oh," she murmured and snuggled up close to him. His arm came automatically around her to draw her closer and she slid two fingers inside his shirt between the buttons.

He didn't seem inclined to object so she decided to try her luck a bit further. She began to nibble at his neck, then his ear, and at the same time tried to ooze onto his lap so that she could wrap her arms around his neck. She thought she was going to get away with it when his hands came out to span her waist. But he picked her up from where she was, already halfway on his lap, and plunked her back down beside him.

"Behave yourself," he said severely.

She was inclined to object, voicing a rebellious "Why?" as she gave a purely feminine flounce beside him. He was going to make a most unmanageable husband, she thought, completely ignoring the fact that she showed no signs of becoming an amenable, tractable wife. The goose doesn't always fancy for herself the sauce she tries to ladle over the gander.

"How did you get mixed up in all of this, Colby? Did MacGuire recruit you after you went to work at the club?" Jase's tone boded ill for Matt if that had been the case.

Colby considered letting Matt take all the blame but knew she couldn't get away with it in the long run. "No," she admitted in a small voice. "It was all my idea. I got the job at the club specifically with that in mind and then went to Matt with the idea. He wasn't too keen on the idea at first. He thought it would be too dange—" Her voice chopped off abruptly.

Jase's eyes glinted silver fire at her. "Go on," he said smoothly. "Too dangerous, I believe you were saying? Don't stop now, Colby. It's just getting interesting." He prodded her ungently in the ribs.

"Yes, well, anyway . . ." She floundered briefly before catching up the thread of her narrative. "Matt thought that since I wasn't a member of the department I wouldn't be of much use, but I . . . er . . . convinced him otherwise."

"I can imagine," Jase agreed sourly. "What did you do? Tell him you were going to do it with or without his sanction so he might as well let you report in to him with whatever information you risked your neck to get?"

She looked at him deadpan for a long moment but couldn't sustain it. "Well, yes, more or less, but he had to admit soon that I was doing the job. I am a good singer, you know," she confided modestly, "and I was—am—a drawing card for the type of patron they want to attract."

"What kind? Sex maniacs? The way you were dressed when I first saw you, they certainly weren't looking to bring in the celibate priests!"

"Certainly not. The club is after the young, rich, idle set who are looking for thrills and excitement." Colby's face was suddenly somber. "That's why I'm doing this. One of my best friends, my roommate at boarding school for five years, got hooked on drugs from that club. She died of an overdose and she was only twenty years old. I'll see those sharks in jail if it's the last thing I do."

It was an infelicitous choice of words. Jase pounced on it like a fish snaps up a hovering insect at feeding time. "No, it won't be the last thing you do because I'm going to make sure it's not. Good God, Colby, you could get killed! Those boys play for keeps. Matthew MacGuire should have his head examined for letting you run such a risk. He should have put you in protective custody or locked you in a padded cell or something. You might have ended up just as dead as your friend. Did your father know about this insane scheme of yours?"

"No, at least I don't think he did at the time, but I rather suspect he might know now, or at least have guessed. I've thought about it and I think that's what's really behind this abduction. I can't think of any other reason he might go to such extremes."

"He's just gone back up in my estimation," Jase announced. "A man of rare good sense. I only wish his daughter had displayed equal intelligence. Well, maybe not. It served its purpose. It got you here in my clutches, and now I'll have the good sense for both of us. We'll go ahead with the wedding plans as soon as we can get a license. I'll let your parents and mine know so they can be here, and the minister can come here too. You're restricted to the ranch until you're safely mine, Colby girl, and that's that."

"Just a blinking minute!" Colby exploded. "Who said I was going to marry an obstinate, bossy man like you anyway?"

"You did, sweetheart," he assured her with smiling certainty. "I don't suppose you'd like to take up where we left off a little while ago?" he continued hopefully. He ran

144

a finger down from her shoulder to track a circle around the nipple that showed so plainly through her thin shirt. "I'm sure I can remember just where I'd got—"

She slapped his hand away smartly. "In a pig's eye!"

"Didn't they teach you a more elegant expression than that at the fancy boarding school you went to all those years? Something from Shakespeare perhaps?"

Colby smiled triumphantly and quoted, " 'It is not a fashion for the maids in France to kiss before they are married.' Shakespeare: *Henry the Fifth.*"

Jase laughed. "I should have known better. Come on, darling. It's time for bed, and since you won't share mine yet, I'll put no more strain on my fast-failing self-control." He stood up and held out his hand.

Colby looked at that powerful, supple hand for a long considering minute and then put her own in it. Jase pulled her to her feet and up against himself, full length and intimately close. Her arms slid around his neck as though pulled upward by puppet strings and she arched into his embrace, not needing the hands that splayed across her hips to mold her to his body. In spite of her apt quotation from Shakespeare, Colby met Jase's kiss with an eagerness and a hungry ardor that matched his own.

"Oh, Colby, if it weren't for the fact that Margy would dent my skull with a frying pan if she found me in bed with you, you wouldn't sleep alone tonight," he told her. "D'you think I could convince her that we were secretly married years ago?" he questioned her whimsically, but the kisses he dropped over her cheeks and eyelids weren't whimsical at all. Things were rapidly getting out of hand again, ably assisted by Colby, when he gritted his teeth and put her from him.

"You're not even trying!" he accused her.

"Oh, yes, I am," she retorted. "I'm trying very hard but you keep having all these noble scruples no matter how I try."

"Saints preserve your virtue, because you're certainly not doing anything about it!" Jase expostulated, exasperated and frustrated.

"Would you like to hear one final quotation?" she smiled sweetly.

"I know I'll regret this, but okay, quote away."

"Voltaire: 'It is one of the superstitions of the human mind to have imagined that virginity could be a virtue.' I've been saving that quotation up for years and this is the first time I've ever had an opportunity to use it," she said smugly.

"I should hope so!" Jase gritted. "My sympathy for your hard-pressed father grows minute by minute. If I turned you over my knee again, I suppose you'd bite me again too?"

She snapped her teeth at him in mute answer. He put his hands on her shoulders and marched her out of the study, carefully locking the door behind them. Their progress back upstairs bore no relation to Colby's cautious descent earlier. Jase flipped light switches on and off with abandon and Colby expected to see Margy pop out of her room at any minute to see what was causing the rumpus, but neither she nor Paul showed signs of stirring.

When Jase stopped outside her door, Colby grumbled, "Margy's some duenna. With all the noise you've been making I would have expected her to be out waving her—frying pan, I think you said it was? Are you trying to get me caught in a compromising situation?"

"Honey," Jase snorted, "if I wanted to compromise you, be sure that I would do a much more thorough job of it than I have done so far! Good night, darling. Sweet dreams."

Colby's look told him that this time, if they were sweet, he would be playing a leading role in them all. She locked her arms around his waist and leaned her head on his chest. He felt so good. "Aren't you going to come tuck me in bed tonight, Jase darling?" she murmured.

"No!" He held her away from him as though she had suddenly burst into flames. "Have a little mercy, Colby. I'm only flesh and blood!"

"Yes . . ." she drawled provokingly. "I know."

He shoved her into her room and nearly bolted down the passage toward his room. She stuck her head out the door and called softly, "Jase." Even at that distance she could see his eyes narrow warily. "I love you. Sweet dreams yourself." She didn't wait to assess his reaction, but popped back into her room and shut her door with a small, definite thud.

It was mean to tease Jase, she knew, but she just couldn't resist it. It was another form of the man-woman thing that had inexplicably sprung to life between them such a short time before. Good heavens, just a little over twenty-four hours ago she hadn't even known he was in the world! And now she'd promised to marry him. Had being kidnapped, manhandled, and nearly seduced addled her brains?

He was practically a stranger, and if anyone had prophesied that she would meet and decide to marry a man she had known little over twenty-four hours, she would have testified for their committal in an institution for the mentally deficient. Just what did she really know about Jase? He was arrogant, pigheaded, had a temper to match her own (and *that* was certainly no plus factor). He had been willing to participate in an illegal abduction, even though from worthy motives, and worst of all, he seemed able to outguess her every move with humiliating ease. Did she really want a husband who could outthink and outmaneuver her?

She was taking off her clothes as these thoughts ran through her mind and she sensuously ran her hands down her sides, past her waist to her hips. Of course, on the plus side, Jase was more than a match for her father. She didn't know why her father had come to Jase in the first place—it was a nagging point she'd lay to rest tomorrow—but Jase would not have agreed to help her father for a discreditable reason. Jase was no man's blind tool. He might do a favor for a friend but he couldn't be coerced into anything. No need to worry about her father being able to run roughshod over Jase.

She stretched out on the bed, the despised nightshirt once again on the floor. Of course there was her physical reaction to Jase, a response no other man had even remotely roused in her. Her breasts were still achingly swollen and she knew that the fires of passion Jase had fanned to blazing life were only lightly banked and would flare again at his arousing touch of her body. She wanted Jase badly, and he so obviously wanted her. Marriage to Jase wouldn't be peaceful, but then, she didn't seem to be a very peaceful person. She and Jase had a lot to learn about each other, the things that only the intimacy of living together could teach them, but she already knew the most important thing: She loved him and he loved her. She'd be a fool to throw that miracle away.

Well, she didn't plan to throw it away—just postpone it a bit. She had to finish what she started. She owed it to Sandi. Jase would understand. He wasn't a person who gave up halfway through, and once the shock of her revelations had had time to subside, he'd let her go back and finish her job. If they couldn't wind up the operation at the club by the end of the month, she'd come back and marry Jase. She wouldn't ask him to wait any longer. She didn't want to wait any longer herself.

She went to sleep a happy woman. She was still smiling when she woke the next morning. It was a glorious day and she could hardly wait to see Jase. She hummed in the shower and dressed with fumble-fingered haste. She wouldn't try to take all her clothes back with her, she decided while she wrestled with suddenly too small buttonholes, just a few of her costumes and some day-clothes to carry her through till the end of the month. One large suitcase ought to do it, she thought, and she could buy whatever else she needed.

She leaped down the stairs two at a time, with all the demented abandon of a mountain goat bounding from crag to crag. Jase was just coming into the lower hall and he watched her precipitous descent with his heart in his mouth. He moved rapidly to the base of the stairs, hoping to break her fall, only to be nearly knocked over when she launched herself at him from the fourth stair from the bottom, leaping confidently into his arms. She rained kisses over his face, which he began to return as soon as he was sure of his balance and breath.

"Good morning, darling," Colby caroled softly, between kisses.

"Yes, isn't it?" Jase chuckled. "And it gets better every minute," he added as he kissed her with enjoyable thoroughness. If he lived to be a hundred, Colby would still manage to surprise and please him. He had thought she might be shy with him, or upset because he wasn't going to let her go back to the club, but her wholehearted enthusiasm belied those fears.

They were thoroughly engrossed in delightful exploration of each other's kissing capabilities when a loud "Ahem," which had been repeated at rapidly lessening intervals, finally registered. Two black heads and bemused gray and violet-blue eyes turned to blankly focus on the foot-tapping Margy who stood five feet away, arms folded and head cocked.

"I . . . er . . . assume that Jase isn't kissing you against your will, Colby?" Margy asked with some asperity.

Colby could feel the heat run up the back of Jase's neck, where her hand rested, and she knew her own face was suffused in a hot blush, but then an irrepressible giggle broke through.

"No," she admitted with a gamine grin. "Fortunately, for the sake of his poor shins, I was cooperating."

"Mmmm. I'd be most interested in hearing how all this peace and goodwill came about. Last night it was daggers drawn, if I recall. Come into the kitchen, children, and have a cup of coffee to cool you down." Margy turned on her heel and led the way.

Jase and Colby followed meekly, hand in hand. Colby peeked up at Jase as he walked beside her and chortled, "You look like a small boy who's been caught stealing cookies or a slice from his mother's newly frosted cake, darling."

Jase grinned back. "I wasn't stealing. What I took is mine." There was a loving, proud possessiveness in his tone that sent an atavistic thrill racing over Colby's skin.

Jase held the door open for her and she preceded him into the kitchen, where Margy was already pouring three cups of coffee. When he had passed through the door as well, he came to Colby's side and laid his arm across her shoulder and escorted her to a chair at the kitchen table. When she sat down, he pulled another chair right next to hers and sat, his thigh in close contact with the length of hers. Margy's eyebrows shot up and she waited pointedly for someone to speak.

Colby and Jase fixed their coffee to their individual tastes, and after his first sip, Jase broke the pregnant silence. "Colby and I are getting married."

Margy didn't look astounded. Being a woman of more than average intelligence, she could read signs held up in front of her nose as well as anyone else. "You relieve my mind," she retorted. "How did all this admirable felicity come about in such a short time?"

"Jase caught me . . . er . . ." Colby faltered slightly.

"Breaking and entering is the term you want, darling," prompted Jase.

"I didn't break anything!" Colby denied heatedly.

"Well, no," Jase admitted, with an obvious effort to be fair. "It was a very professional job of lockpicking. You didn't even scratch the lock plate."

Margy started laughing. "Now that sounds much more normal for you two! So Jase caught you in his study last night?"

"Yes." Colby wrinkled her nose at him. "He was lying in wait like an ogre in his lair."

"And . . ." Margy prompted when neither of the two principals seemed inclined to elaborate further.

"She wanted to use the phone," Jase added helpfully.

"And . . ." Margy said again.

Jase and Colby exchanged glances. Colby nodded slightly in resignation. She guessed Margy would have to know the bare outlines. She certainly wasn't going to let it lie without further elaboration.

"Colby was a narc, an undercover narcotics agent, working on an investigation at the club where she sang," Jase said tightly. The risks she had been running still had the power to send cold chills down his back, even now when he had her safely by his side. "She was trying to get in touch with the police lieutenant who's in charge. She got a partial call through to him during the flight out here and wanted an uninterrupted one." The brusque words spoke volumes.

Colby's eyebrows had expressed surprise at Jase's use of the past tense when he described her activities at the club, and they didn't return to normal position when Margy questioned her in astonishment, "Are you a police officer, Colby?"

"I am not an official member of the department," Colby answered carefully. "I am merely assisting the investigation in a civilian capacity. I don't plan to make this sort of thing a life career, but there are special circumstances in this case that have given me a personal interest. I lost a very dear friend because of the people who are behind the ring we're hoping to break up."

Now it was Jase's turn for his eyebrows to register displeasure at Colby's choice of verb tense, and her obvious emphasis on the present tense was bringing his eyebrows into a scowling black line. His voice, however, was smooth as he said, "It dawned on me last night, Colby, my devious darling, that I never actually heard you promise you'll give up the idea of going back to the club before we marry. I'd like your word now, Colby."

There was unmistakable authority and demand in Jase's voice and Margy looked at Colby. What Margy saw on that lovely face made her hastily gather up the coffee cups and move them out of range. Colby didn't move away from Jase physically, but suddenly she seemed to withdraw to a far distant place. Her eyes turned a storm dark blue and her delectable chin jutted into a fighting tilt.

"I thought you understood, Jase. I must go back. Matt needs the information I can get for him. It will ruin months of careful work if we can't be ready when the next shipment comes in, and we may never have such a good chance to catch all the big sharks as well as the little fish." Her voice was quiet but resolute.

"I promise you that I will come back to you at the end of the month. If we aren't able to close down the operation on this try, I'll give over my part of the investigation. Just two weeks, Jase, that's all I'm asking for."

Jase didn't even have to consider her plea. "No." The flat negative allowed for no appeal or argument. "You're out of it and out of it you'll stay. We'll get a license and be married three days from now. I want your parole, Colby, and we'll go into town and start the paperwork." He smiled lovingly at her, sure that she'd recognize the futility of further resistance.

Margy was glad she'd had the foresight to move the coffee cups from range when Colby's hand groped automatically for a handy missile. "No parole, Jase Culhane!" Colby yelled. "I'm going to go back and finish what I started. You are the most refractory, intractable, pertinacious mule I have ever met, and I'll get away from this ranch even if you keep me bound and gagged, locked in a cellar! I'll—I'll hop all the way to town, wherever it is!" And with that, Colby stormed out of the kitchen.

The two remaining people sat in silence while the echoes of the door slam died away. Margy drew in a deep breath and said mildly, "Does this mean the wedding is off?"

"No!" Jase said forcefully. "She may come to it kicking and screaming or maybe even bound and gagged, but I'm going to marry that little wildcat in three days, with or without her consent. I'll send one of the boys into town to pay the license fee and fill in the paper work. I can arrange it with the county clerk, Ted Brown, over the phone and he'll pull all the right strings for me. I won't risk taking Colby off the ranch until we're married, and I'm going to have to stay around to keep an eye on her. No telling what she'll try next."

He raked a distracted hand through his black hair. Margy watched him with mingled amusement and compassion. Poor Jase! "Would it really be so bad to let her go back and finish her job, Jase? It seems to mean a lot to her."

"It could mean her life," he answered harshly. "She got into it because of some crazy idea of avenging her friend's death from an overdose of drugs, but I won't let her go back and run the risk of getting that lovely throat cut. Those boys play dirty, Margy. Colby's way out of her league, and if she doesn't recognize it, I do! And so does her father. Colby thinks, and I do too, that he found out about this harebrained scheme of hers and that's why he arranged all of this. Whether that's at the bottom of it or not, she's safe now and I intend to keep her that way. She loves me and I love her and she'll marry me."

Jase got up and stalked over to the kitchen door. He looked out of the glass set into its upper half and saw Colby, flanked by his two dogs, leaning over a corral fence, rubbing the ears and noses of the horses that jostled to get near her. He judged she would stay there for a while, probably maligning him to the patient, sympathetic ears of the animals, safely out of immediate trouble.

"I'm going to make some phone calls, Margy. Can you fry some bacon and scramble up some eggs and bring it to me in the study? I have a feeling I'd better keep my strength up." While he was speaking, Jase was pouring himself another cup of coffee, and at Margy's cheerful assent, he headed toward his study, cup in hand.

Jase was right. The dogs and horses were getting quite an earful about Colby's current opinion of his character. Deep in her mind she knew Jase was only doing this for her own good and because he was worried about her safety, but it didn't mitigate her fury. She wasn't in any frame of mind to be reasonable—what woman in a temper ever is?—and it was as much determination to 'show' Jase as it was to finish her job which fueled her contumacy.

If she only had an idea in which direction town lay, she'd be off in a second, she fumed. She turned away from the horses and glared at the house. *Wouldn't I just love to be able to show you, Jase Culhane,* she thought scathingly. Suddenly she went board-rigid, and her eyes widened at an astounding thought.

What a dunce she was! What a fatuous moron! The telephone! It had been there all along. There was a telephone, therefore there had to be telephone lines, which, if followed, would eventually lead her to civilization. Even a child would have thought of it sooner.

There were several dirt roads leading away from the ranch house in different directions, including the one that led to the airstrip, but all seemed equally traveled, with nothing to indicate which one led to civilization. Telephone lines were directional. They eventually had to lead to somewhere she wanted to go, be it a town or another ranch house where she could use a phone.

Her stomach rumbled. It reminded her that she had a long ride ahead of her and she'd best lay her plans carefully, and that included not fainting from hunger on the trail. She hoped Jase wasn't still in the kitchen. He might really be able to read her mind, and while she was sure he wouldn't go so far as to rip down all the phone lines, he might confine her to the house.

She was a singer. Could she also be an actress, or at least enough of one to fool Margy? She headed back to the house. When she went back into the kitchen, much less precipitately than she had gone out, she found Margy just finishing up Jase's bacon and eggs. With a pretty apology for subjecting Margy to the scene between Jase and herself, she was able to coax Margy into giving her Jase's portion, which she consumed while Margy made another batch for Jase. While Margy cooked and Colby ate, Colby determined Jase's whereabouts. She then cunningly informed Margy that she was going to her room and to tell Jase she'd be down for lunch or maybe dinner, but that she was going to read a book or take a nap and she didn't have anything further to say to him.

Margy grinned and decided she'd tell Jase that, even though Colby had simmered down a little, perhaps he'd best leave bad enough alone and let the cooling-off process proceed a little further before risking his shins to Colby's untender mercies once more.

As soon as Margy disappeared, bearing Jase's breakfast tray, Colby whipped into the pantry and filched a hanging salami, a large chunk of cheese, a loaf of rye bread, and one of several bottles of mineral water she had seen on the shelf. The study was on the opposite side of the house and had no clear view of the saddling barn. Colby was across the open space like a streak of light, accompanied by the gamboling dogs, who thought a run was just the thing. Their goddess was happy again!

Colby ducked into the shelter of the barn. As she had hoped, all the men were out working and she was unobserved. She hurried to the tack room and pulled down a saddle and bridle and set of saddlebags. She could ride bareback, but she was out of condition for a really long ride, and she'd probably have to spend the night on the trail. A blanket, even one that smelled of horse, would be welcome. She went out the back way, carrying the saddle and other accoutrements, including the now reassuringly loaded saddlebag.

A low crooning call brought every horse within hearing at a raking trot, and she chose a powerful bay gelding and began to saddle him expertly. Babe nickered disconsolately and Merlin butted her in the back with equine insistence when she led out the bay. In spite of these hazards she finished with the gelding in record time. She swung up on his back, settling herself and testing his mouth with practiced hands. He took the bit eagerly but with easy manners. He had the look of endurance, which was why she had chosen him over Babe, who was sweet but had been chosen primarily with her suitability for a beginner in mind.

She ordered the dogs back to the house and saw them obey with reluctance. Jase might suspect her sooner if the dogs weren't waiting for him in their accustomed places, and she couldn't take them with her anyway. Keeping the saddling barn between herself and the house, she marked the direction of the telephone lines and began a wide circle away from the house, intending to pick them up when she was out of sight of the house.

Once she was safely lost to view, she put the bay to a ground-eating pace and picked up the line where it was strung between convenient trees, or, lacking trees, man-erected poles. She and the horse settled down to cover as much ground as possible.

In the study Jase had completed the first of his calls, to his satisfaction, when Margy tapped on the door. He opened the door for her and relieved her of the appetizingly laid tray. She followed him into the room and he looked questioningly at her. "All quiet?"

"Reasonably so," she answered, a small smile quirking at the corners of her mouth. "Colby came back in the house, ate your breakfast, and went upstairs. She said something about reading a book and that she might be back down for lunch or dinner, but that she had nothing further to say to you."

"Hmmm. Do you think that might qualify as an improvement? I mean on the theory of if you can't say something nice to someone say nothing at all?" Jase's grin was wry.

"Oh, I imagine you'll still find plenty of areas of communication," Margy reassured him teasingly. "Enjoy your breakfast, Jase."

"Thanks, Margy."

He sat back at his desk and, while he ate, consulted an index file until he had the number he required. While he listened to the ringing, Jase forked up the last few bites of eggs. He wasn't looking forward to his next phone call, but he had a feeling that the man on the other end of the line was going to enjoy it even less.

Only three were present for lunch. Paul seated Margy

courteously while Jase stood waiting to take his own seat. Paul looked around curiously, noting no place was laid for Colby. When Margy began to serve the vegetables, Paul said with bewilderment, "Isn't Colby back yet? I mean I thought since you're here, Jase . . ." His voice trailed off as Margy and Jase stared at him.

"Back from where, Paul?" Jase asked in dangerously calm tones.

"Well, from your ride this morning," said a now throughly confused young man.

"Our ride *when* this morning?" Jase's voice had a hoarse, strained note.

"Soon after breakfast," Paul responded concisely. He could pick up a nuance as well as his grandmother. "I was taking a break from my lessons and I looked out the window just in time to see Colby disappearing in the trees, heading west toward Black's Leap. I—I just assumed you were right in front of her. She was on Barney. I recognized him from those two white hind stockings, you know." He went on more thoughtfully, "Come to think of it, I didn't see the dogs trailing either, and of course, they're out by the back door as always. I saw them when I came in earlier."

Jase was out of the room as the last words hung in the air. They heard the thud of his steps as he took the stairs three at a time. Margy shook her head dolefully. "It's my fault. I told him she went upstairs so he didn't check on her during the morning. She must have just gone right back outside when I took him breakfast in the study. Paul, go tell whoever's at the stables to saddle up Merlin, or if no one's there, do it yourself. When that's done, bring me a saddle pack. I'll be making up a food packet. I don't

159

imagine Jase will be in for dinner tonight and he'll be eating lunch in the saddle."

Paul left on a dead run, but Margy didn't even think of reproving him. She left lunch cooling on the table and bustled into the kitchen where she began to assemble food-stuffs with the deftness of long practice. By the time Jase came back downstairs, she was putting the finishing touches on a packet of sandwiches and had a Thermos of hot coffee filled and capped.

Jase and Paul entered the kitchen at the same time, from different directions, and Paul blurted hastily, "Merlin's saddled. Barney's still out." He tossed the saddlebags he had slung over his arm onto the kitchen table where Margy received them and swiftly began to pack.

"Thanks, Paul," Jase acknowledged. He was grim-faced and drawn. He was also dressed for hard riding in service-able jeans, denim shirt and wearing a denim jacket. He carried a sweat-stained, well-used Stetson and a tightly wrapped bedroll and sleeping bag. He scanned the pile of food Margy was hastily stowing away and grabbed a sand-wich before Margy could whisk it out of sight.

"I knew I was going to need a good breakfast," he mumbled as he bit into the soft bread. When he had finished chewing, before he took another bite, he added to Paul, "Get my rifle and scabbard out of the gun room, Paul, and a box of cartridges. Also get the trail first-aid kit. You know where it's stowed."

He finished the sandwich and practically poured down the glass of icy cold milk Margy handed him silently. "I'm sorry, Jase," she apologized softly. "I should have watched her up the stairs."

"No, Margy, it's my fault. I should have chained her to my wrist." His face was hard and determined. "Be assured

I won't make that mistake again. Don't worry if we don't come back in tonight. If something goes wrong, I'll send one of the dogs back for help. She's a damn fine rider, though, and Barney's a good horse for the trail." He laughed. "I imagine that's why she picked him out. It may take me a while to catch up with her, and I'm sure she's making the most of her lead."

"But, Jase," Margy protested, "she doesn't know where she's going. There's only wild country past Black's Leap."

"Of course she knows where she's going. She'll be heading straight toward Dog Creek as the crow flies," he said with weary confidence. "Colby wouldn't have taken off if she didn't know where to go. She was mad, but it didn't make her stupid. She only headed toward Black's Leap because the barn shielded her from sight of the house in that direction. You can be sure that as soon as she hit the trees she turned back and picked up the line of the phone wires. She'll follow them right downtown, or rather she would, except that I'll catch up to her before she gets that far. Barney's a good trail horse, but he's not a patch on Merlin."

He shook his head. "In fact I wonder why she didn't just take Merlin. She'd know he was by far the best horse."

"Take Merlin?" Margy gasped. "Merlin doesn't let anyone but you on his back, Jase."

Jase snorted. "Merlin would lie down and let Colby make him into a rug if she took the notion. I forgot, you've not seen her effect on dumb animals—and some who are purportedly not so dumb either. If it weren't for the fact that the men know I'd personally take each one of them apart if they helped her, she'd have had an honor guard to escort her off the ranch with one flicker of those long eyelashes."

161

Margy and Paul watched Jase knee Merlin into a ground-eating canter. He didn't even bother to track Colby directly, so certain was he that he'd pick up her trail near the phone lines, out of sight of the house. Kelpie and Lije bounded eagerly in Merlin's track.

Colby was discovering that one does not forget how to ride, but one's muscles may well forget the stresses imposed by long unaccustomed hours in the saddle, particularly those muscles anatomically dubbed gluteus. To put it bluntly, she was not going to be particularly comfortable sitting for some time to come once she finished this grueling ride.

As yet the discomfort was only a vague twinge, but she knew that as the hours sped onward the twinge would become an uncomfortable ache and eventually a teeth-gritting stiffness. After all, one does not normally embark on an extended trail ride when one hasn't been in the saddle for several years, except for a one-hour ride on a mare with a rocking-chair gait.

It was a temptation to push the horse, but Colby knew realistically that she wouldn't make the town she felt sure she was heading toward in one day. She contented herself with a steady pace, which she judged she and the horse could maintain for the long hours without unduly stressing either of them. She knew, resignedly, however, which of them was going to be in better shape by the time this trek was done. The horse was used to it; she surely wasn't.

A dirt road crossed and recrossed her path numerous times and she was heartened. It must be the road into town, thus bearing out her deductions. She chose, however, to stay with those thin threads of wire, stretching across the rolling grasslands and through the wooded areas. The wire would be strung in the shortest distance possible and she might cut off miles if she followed its path, rather than the easier but longer one of the road.

Once she was fairly away from the main ranch, Colby spared a thought to Jase and his reaction. There was no blinking at it. He was going to be furious. Well, fair was fair. She wasn't too pleased with him right then herself.

It was sad to state, but Jase was partially correct in his initial assessment of Colby's character. She had been spoiled, not by a *doting* father, but by her proven ability to stand up to her *overwhelming* father. It had made her overly fond of having her own way and she was so used to fighting for her independence that she tended to fight first and ask if it was really necessary afterward. Without this preconditioned habit, she might have listened to Jase with an open mind, instead of rejecting out of hand his arbitrary decree that she retire to the sidelines for her safety's sake.

In a cooler moment Colby might have admitted that her chances of safely taking up her investigative role were pretty much nonexistent. Her father's Machiavellian strategy had probably accomplished the ruin of her care-fully nurtured cover, not through exposure, but simply by indicating to what lengths this powerful man was willing to go to sever his daughter's association with the club. The owners of the club might appreciate her drawing power, but never to the extent that they would continue to with-stand a determined Steven Duncan and all the resources at his command.

Still, it was not in Colby's nature to give up. She was, after all, Steven Duncan's daughter and she'd give it her best shot. When she got to wherever these wires were leading her, she'd finally have an uninterrupted conversa-tion with Matt and decide where to go from there. If Matt

163

could honestly tell her that she'd do more harm than good by coming back, she'd resign herself to the inevitable and accept that her father's king-size spanner in the works was irreparably damaging. Then she'd have to go back to the ranch and make her peace with Jase, and that was going to be no easy task. She shuddered slightly.

She stopped once by a running, shallow stream to water the horse. It looked clean and was deliciously chill, but her city habits of distrusting water that doesn't come certified safe from a tap kept her from sampling it along with her thirsty horse. She let him drink a small amount and then pulled him away. He wasn't blown but she judged it wiser to let him drink his fill in stages. She slipped his bit to enable him to graze easily, and while he cropped contentedly nearby, she made a hasty nooning herself.

The salami was hard to break into chunks and the cheese tended to crumble, but she was ravenous so she managed. The bread wiped up most of the grease from the salami and a dabble in the stream took care of the rest. She splashed water over her face and throat as well. She wished she had a hat, and she was sure her nose was getting sunburned, but there wasn't much she could do about either.

She broached the bottle of mineral water and drank sparingly. There seemed to be plenty of streams so if she went through all of the water she carried she wouldn't die of thirst, but it still seemed a good idea to conserve her supplies.

Colby groaned softly when she levered herself up from the ground. It was a great temptation to curl up in the soft grass for a short nap, but she knew she didn't dare. She walked around to loosen the stiffness that had set in during her brief rest and to ease that feeling of incipient bowleggedness that comes to those who havent't ridden regularly in a while.

For the first time since she had ridden away from the house, she really took note of the land she rode through. It was empty. There had been wildlife in plenty, but of humankind, no sign or hand except the wire. Jase had said isolated, but suddenly the reality behind the words was apparent. She had left one island of humanity and was riding toward another, but in between there was only herself. Tonight, in the darkness, there would be only herself.

There would be the horse, of course, and she really didn't fear marauding animals, but she had never been so totally alone before in her life. In the city or tamer country there was the telephone or neighbors for succor. It wasn't, she realized, that she feared the solitude, merely that she realized her inexperience had left her unfitted for coping alone with the myriad emergencies that could arise swiftly in such a situation.

When she married Jase, she would have much to learn if she wished to share his life fully. He was basically a man of open spaces, although she knew he would have no awe of cities. Could she adapt herself to a primarily rural life? If she wanted Jase she would have to, she concluded. A reminiscent grin curled her mouth. He'd make it worth her while.

She let the horse drink his fill, replaced the bit, and swung up into the saddle with most of the lithe grace she had previously shown. It was doubtful whether she would still be able to do the same tomorrow morning. By then it would probably be a painful clamber!

By the time the sun was beginning to drop measurably in the sky, Colby was definitely feeling the effect of her ride

165

and concluding that perhaps she might even have acted somewhat hastily. The fury directed at Jase, which had given her impetus, had largely drained away and the oncoming night was looming darker and lonelier each minute. And Jase was going to be very, very angry with her. She wondered if he'd discovered her flight by now.

A horrible thought struck her. What if he thought she was lost? He'd be worried sick if he believed she'd ridden off into the wilderness with no fixed destination in mind. When he discovered that she was gone, he'd have every man out looking for her. Vivid scenarios of Margy distrait, Paul upset, and Jase afraid for her safety began to unfold themselves in her imagination and Colby began to comprehend the cost to others of her impulsive actions.

With that realization Colby took a large step forward in maturity. From a one-sided viewpoint, her inner vision suddenly expanded to include the needs and reactions of other people who loved her and claimed the right to her consideration through that love.

It was a new concept for her. Her relationship with her parents had not been such that she had ever considered this factor before. Her mother was not a particularly maternal woman and the years away at boarding school had stretched the mother-daughter ties thin. Committees and commissions were her mother's métier, not motherhood. Her father would have been quick to turn any yielding on her part to his own purposes, and there was no one she had been close enough to otherwise—except for Sandi, and Sandi was dead.

Colby pulled the horse to a halt. There was someone now. She loved Jase and he loved her. Her first loyalty was to him. If she could have carried through her part in Matt's investigation, she would have, but Colby knew her usefulness there was ended. Her father had seen to that. She would have put Jase through agony for nothing, out of temper and a desire to pay him back for things that were basically not his fault.

She turned the bay's head and headed him back in the direction from which she had just come. She couldn't reach the ranch tonight, but she was going back.

CHAPTER SEVEN

Colby had been retracing her outward trail for over an hour when her horse suddenly lifted his head and nickered shrilly. There was an unexpected, answering bugle and Colby's head jerked upward in shock. She was so tired by now that she hadn't really paid attention to anything except to be sure she was keeping on her previous track.

It was late afternoon and when she looked in the direction of that bugle of sound the low-sinking sun dazzled her eyes for a moment. She blinked rapidly and shaded her tired eyes.

Jase had pulled Merlin to a halt and ordered the dogs down. He had seen Colby making her way back along the track some time before, and he waited for her to see him. As he had watched her weary figure coming toward him, a wellspring of thanksgiving bubbled up. She had been riding back to him. He didn't know yet why she had changed her mind, but she had been riding toward the ranch, no longer away from it.

When Merlin answered Barney's neigh, Jase watched Colby's dawning awareness. He was still too far away to see her expression, but a new vitality straightened her spine and suddenly Barney was galloping toward him. He dismounted and stepped away from Merlin.

Colby pulled her horse to a halt as she reached Jase and threw herself into his arms, much as she had from the stairs that morning. She was hot, sweaty, and dust-smudged but none of it mattered. Jase's arms closed tightly around her and hers wrapped around his waist as she burrowed into his chest.

"Oh, Jase, I'm sorry. I'm sorry," she said penitently. "It was childish and futile and I do love you so. I'm sorry for worrying you and Margy and Paul. Are you very angry with me?"

Since she kept her head buried in his chest during this whole speech, it was rather incoherent in spots, but Jase was able to decipher the majority of it. He smiled down tenderly at the dusty black head, but his voice betrayed little of that soft expression.

"I ought to beat you, Colby," he said sternly.

"I know," she agreed submissively, causing him to smile broadly. Then she leaned back in his arms to meet his eyes fairly and he tried to school his expression to sternness. "I think, however, you'll have to wait until I get over the effects of this ride. I already feel as though I've been worked over with a large stick, and I shudder to think what I'm going to feel like tomorrow. You don't happen to have a portable hot tub of water with you, do you? I think I'd like to soak for hours in a steaming tub."

She smiled winningly up at him. He couldn't be too angry, the strength of his clasp and the way he had held out his arms to her as she came off the horse and into his ready embrace told her that.

She pulled her arms from around his waist and slid them up his chest to stroke the sides of his neck and tug his head down for a kiss. He resisted for a moment, but

169

finally a smile broke through his mock sternness and he captured her mouth with firm mastery.

When he lifted his head again, he looked down at her quizzically. "Are you trying to get 'round me, Colby? Is this a display of feminine wiles designed to defuse my righteous wrath?"

"And if I say yes, what will you do?" she queried him, unabashed by his steady regard, especially since his hands were stroking up and down her spine as he spoke with such pseudogravity.

"Why, just enjoy it, I imagine," he drawled and pulled her more tightly to him. "I was very, very angry, you know, so you'll have to put a lot of effort into placating me."

She drooped her eyelashes disconsolately. "My, my, that sounds like a long assignment. I don't know if I'll have the strength for such an arduous task." She peeped up at him through her lashes and said solemnly, "Of course, if I were to have some food to give me energy . . ." She let her words trail off suggestively.

"Didn't you manage to steal some food to bring with you?" he asked without a trace of sympathy.

"Of course I did," she retorted sharply. "I'm not such an idiot that I'd start out on such a long ride without some food and water."

"You were an idiot for starting out on the ride at all," he riposted. "And if you manage to kick me in the shins, Colby, I'll tan your rear for sure, even if I have to hold you down and gag you first."

Colby carefully set down the foot she had lifted and drawn back when Jase called her an idiot. She might be an idiot, but not that big of a one! She assumed a dignified mien and wiggled slightly for release. "I have apologized," she said stiffly, "and I consider that I had more than ample provocation for my actions." She wiggled again, harder this time.

"If you keep wiggling like that," he said dryly, "I'll consider that I've had more than ample provocation for what I'm going to do to you next."

Since he had also pulled her firmly against his lower body as he spoke, the import of his implied threat was startlingly clear. Colby subsided immediately.

"Have I, at last, found the way to make you behave? I don't know whether to be relieved or affronted that the threat of making love to you should have such immediate salutory results." His voice shook with suppressed laughter.

"Well, to threaten to make love to me is one thing, but to promise to make love to me is another thing entirely," she responded demurely.

Jase laughed again. "Enough of this suggestive repartee. I know a good place a mile back to make camp for the night. There's a stream and good grazing for the horses and firewood close by. The stream isn't heated, but you can brave the chill and splash if you wish. You are definitely grubby, my darling, and your nose is sunburned. I might even be prevailed upon to share a sandwich with you if you ask me nicely enough, and for a kiss, you might get a fairly warm cup of coffee."

Colby groaned loudly as she hoisted herself onto her horse. "What do I have to give you to get some liniment?"

He snapped his fingers. "I knew that there was something I forgot to bring along. I could give you a thorough massage, though, guaranteed to be just the thing to loosen up those sore muscles," he offered straight-faced.

Colby judged it wiser to let that last offer pass unremarked, and besides, her discomfort had now reached an acute stage. She had been in the saddle for the better (or worse, from her point of view) part of the seven hours, and her body was letting her know, in no uncertain terms, its opinion of such activities.

Jase must have understood her discomfort because he kept the pace steady but not uncomfortably fast. He also didn't require her to make conversation, for which she was grateful. Words sound strange when they are forced from between clenched teeth, and Colby's teeth were certainly clenched.

Jase led on Merlin and soon he turned aside from the line of wire to angle off toward a stand of trees, similar to many she had passed, that usually denoted the presence of water. He stopped before he rode among them and dismounted in the shin-high yellowing grass.

He walked over to Colby and held up his arms to clasp her around her waist and ease her down. She came down with more grace than a sack of meal, but less than that of a practiced equestrienne. "We'll make camp out in the open. There's a stream about twenty yards into those trees where you can clean up and cool off. The water's safe to drink too. I didn't bring you any clean clothes, but here's a towel at least. I'll start camp and see to the horses." He looked her over critically. "I think you'll just about manage yourself."

"I could do it if I had to," she informed him with a small spark of vigor.

"I know you could, honey," he assured her gently, correctly assessing the tired smudges under her eyes and the stiffness and effort with which she moved, "but you don't have to. You've had a rough few days, one way and another, and I'm here now." He turned her in the direction of the trees and gave her a slight starting push.

Colby went without further demur, one hand carrying the towel Jase had provided, the other pushing the branches of the trees out of her path. When she reemerged considerably later, she had removed most of the surface dirt and, even though she had had to resume the same clothes, she felt reasonably presentable.

The camp was transformed. Jase had flattened an area of grass, unsaddled and cared for the horses, spread the saddle blankets to air, and made a seat and backrest out of the saddles and sleeping bag. A small fire crackled cheerfully in a ring of stones, and there was a can of water heating to the side of the direct flames. Jase was nowhere in sight, but moments later he came out of the trees himself, carrying an armload of wood.

"Feeling better now, darling?" He dumped the load of wood on top of a smaller pile. "You look better," he added candidly.

"If you really love me, don't show me a mirror!" she retorted from her heart. She had a very good idea of what she had looked like, and even how she looked now.

He just chuckled and indicated the seat he had devised for her comfort. "Do you think you could bear to sit down again, or would you rather stand for a bit longer? The coffee in the Thermos is reasonably warm and you can eat your sandwich either sitting or standing, as milady prefers."

Colby laid an experimental hand on her buttocks and tested the extent of the damage, much as she had after Jase had walloped her. The rueful thought crossed her mind that certain parts of her anatomy were faring very badly in this adventure. "I think I'll stand for a while longer, thank you very kindly," she grimaced. "I'm still trying to convince my legs that they aren't permanently bent into the shape of that horse's barrel."

"You'll have to sit sometime," he advised her with scant sympathy, "unless you plan to sleep standing up like the horses."

"I know," she sighed in agreement, "but I'm putting off the evil minute as long as I can."

Jase handed her a cup full of surprisingly hot coffee and a somewhat battered sandwich. In spite of its rather flattened appearance, it was delicious, Colby decided as she chewed the roast beef and Swiss cheese. The sharp bite of the Dijon mustard made her salivary glands perk up and she finished off the whole sandwich in record time. She looked hopefully at Jase.

"Would you like a hard-boiled egg?" he asked her politely.

"Several," she responded. "I'm starved."

"I can see you're not going to be a cheap wife to feed," he said sorrowfully as he peeled and salted one egg for her, and then a second. "Would you like something else, Colby darling?"

Colby chewed and swallowed the second egg. "Is there something else?"

"Certainly," Jase assured her dryly. "You can have your breakfast now or in the morning. It's up to you. There wasn't time for Margy to pack a full-course dinner, you know." He poured out some dry dog food for the two patient dogs as he spoke and at his gesture Lije and Kelpie came forward to eat their own meal.

"We could finish the rest of my salami and cheese and bread," she offered magnanimously. "Do you have a knife? It's rather hard to break off chunks of the salami. It bends."

Jase made a muffled choking sound as he rummaged in his jacket pocket and pulled out a clasp knife. Colby looked at him with a scowl but knew she wasn't in a position to retaliate. Remembering her efforts to section the salami earlier, her own mouth curved into a smile.

They finished the last of the salami and cheese, sitting side by side, leaning against the saddles. Colby had lowered herself gingerly to the ground and discovered that if she rocked back on her spine and flexed her knees she wasn't too uncomfortable. Any posture expert would have remonstrated in horror at the curvature of her spine, but it was the most comfortable position she could achieve, and she was content.

Jase had eaten his own sandwich and eggs and they had shared the salami, cheese and bread equally. Then he made fresh instant coffee, using the water he had heated, and with dried creamer and sugar it was deliciously palatable. The dogs lay at their feet and the horses cropped contentedly nearby. When Jase's arm came around Colby's shoulders, she fitted herself closely to his side with a wordless murmur of satisfaction. The open, unpeopled spaces were friendly with Jase by her side. Had she faced this night alone, they would have been at least alien, if not hostile.

The evening star showed through a rent in the darkening blue velvet of the sky, and soon other small stars picked their own holes in night's fabric. Colby was cat-content, curled up against Jase's warm, strong body. When he spoke, his voice was gentle.

"You were riding back to the ranch, Colby."

It wasn't said as a question, but she knew it required an answer. "I was coming back to you, Jase," she affirmed.

He sighed. "That means a lot, Colby. Thank you."

There was a long companionable silence. Jase was content to hold Colby close to his side, savoring the knowledge that she was safe and she was his. Colby shifted slightly, easing her stiffening muscles, and he could feel a throaty chuckle work its way up through her rib cage.

"I still don't know where your ranch is, Jase. Do you think you might finally tell me just where I'm going to spend my married life?"

She should have known better than to give him such a perfect opening. "That's easy, Colby," his teasing tone forewarned her. "In my bed, in my arms, and in my heart. That's where you'll spend your life from now on."

"Jase." She tried to sound stern, but failed lamentably. That was just where she wanted to be.

He squeezed her shoulders slightly and relented. "You'll live in the Land of the Shining Mountains, Colby, or perhaps you prefer calling it the Treasure State?" She jabbed him ungently in the ribs with a stiffened forefinger. "Okay, okay." He patted the ground on which they sprawled. "This is Montana and if you'd kept going another fifteen miles, you'd have ridden right down the main street of Dog Creek."

"Dog Creek?" she questioned, slightly incredulous.

"Dog Creek," he affirmed. "It's not big but it's friendly." He spoke seriously then. "It'll be a good life, Colby. I promise you. You won't regret trusting yourself to my keeping and I'll hold you safe and happy all of my life."

It had to be said. She owed Jase total honesty. With a painful effort Colby pulled away from him and tucked her legs beneath her, tailor fashion. She picked up one of his hands and held it in both of hers, seeking courage.

"Jase," she said in a low voice, "I love you, more than I thought myself capable of loving another human being, so I have to be totally honest with you. If I thought there was a chance of my being able to continue being useful at the club, I would still be riding for that town, Dog Creek, and its telephones. You must understand and accept that. It was an obligation I assumed before I met you and I would, if I could, complete it to the best of my ability. Sandi was my friend and she didn't deserve to die at twenty years of age, her life untasted and futile. The men who are responsible for that death and countless other wrecked lives are evil men. I would have a personal hand in their punishment if I could. I shan't forgive my father for wrecking my chance at that and perhaps Matt's whole investigation, whatever his motives. I'm an adult. He had no right to interfere. It was my choice.

"You must accept that about me. I carry through, to the best of my ability, whatever I take on." Jase stirred restlessly and she squeezed his hand before she continued. "I realized that my father had made it impossible for me to continue at the club simply because the people who are behind the club can't afford to associate with people who might make waves, and my father has raised an oceanful of them. They won't have me back, and if I try to press the issue, I'll do more harm than good.

"I really knew that before I left this morning; I think I knew it from the moment the plane took off. But I have a beastly temper," she said, feeling rather than hearing Jase's light laugh, "and when you gave me no chance to make my own decision about going back this morning, just like my father would have done, I acted before I thought. You were my father all over again, Jase, and I reacted just like I do with him."

"What? I am not your father, Colby!" Jase expostulated in scandalized tones.

Colby giggled helplessly. "I think I phrased that badly," she admitted.

"You certainly did!"

She tried to explain more clearly. "I've had to fight my father all my life, Jase. He loves me, in his own way, but it doesn't stop him from trying to use me toward his own ends. Barry Delaroy is a case in point." Jase stiffened; she could feel it through the hand she still clasped tightly. She hurried on. "It's just that I've got into the habit of fighting for my independence, even when it's neither necessary nor . . . desirable." Her voice dropped on this last word.

She fell silent. There wasn't really anything more to say on her part. It was up to him now. Could he accept her revelation that, were it possible, she would go back to the club, setting aside their love for a time? Jase was a proud, possessive man. He would require that his wife put him first before all things, as he would put her first.

She loved Jase and was secure in the knowledge of his love for her, but there was more than love in the building of a life together. There had to be liking as well, and a blending of inner harmony. The basic goals had to be similar, complementary. She and Jase had had no time to delve into such matters. They fought, they loved. Could they marry with no more than that between them?

" 'I could not love thee, dear, so much, loved I not honour more. . . .' I understand, Colby darling." Jase's voice was thoughtful as he quoted. "I understand about your father too. I owed him a favor, for my father's sake, and he used that moral debt to accomplish his own ends.

But I can't say I regret the outcome in the slightest. It brought me you, and the greatest happiness I'll ever know to have you for my wife."

Colby thrilled to the simple assurance in his calm voice. Jase continued. "I understand. Now you must understand. If you could go back to finish up your part in the investigation, I would fight to keep you here, even if it meant locking you in your room at the ranch. I would just have to depend on your eventual forgiveness, but I would keep you here with me, safe. Perhaps I am like your father in that respect, but to keep you unharmed, I would outrage your sense of independence. Can you accept that about me?"

"But what if the situations were reversed? Would you forgive me if I locked you up to keep you safe?" Colby had released his hand and now sat chin in hands, elbows resting on her knees.

"D'you think you could manage to lock me up?" he asked straight-faced.

"Be serious," Colby said tartly. "It's the principle of the thing, and you know it!"

"I know, sweetheart. I've never really thought about it before, Colby, in relation to a woman I love, first of all because I've never been in love before, and then, I never expected to fall in love with someone who casually risks her life the way you seem willing to do."

"It isn't casual at all!" she replied heatedly. "I considered the risks and decided they were acceptable. There really wasn't any danger as long as I wasn't suspected, and I never actively sought information by breaking in offices or such. I'm not the only woman undercover agent Matt has, you know."

179

"You're the only one I'm in love with," he retorted with finality.

She watched him rake a hand through his hair, a sure sign of agitation. "Look, Colby, we're just going to have to agree to disagree on this point and hope the situation never arises again. Chauvinistic or not, I'll protect the woman I love to the best of my ability when and where I feel necessary. You can do your best to thwart me, though I hope I'll be able to keep you by my side with less drastic measures than I have had to use so far."

She saw the white gleam of his smile and smiled herself. She had a very good idea of the less drastic means he planned to use in the future, and she wondered if he also had considered that such methods were apt to be susceptible to use by both parties concerned. Well, as he said, they'd just have to hope such a situation would never arise, and her undercover days were over anyway. Perhaps not the most satisfactory conclusion to a difference of opinion on principle, but certainly the most practical.

She curled up next to him again, smiling a small woman-smile that he couldn't see. Jase was too wise to believe that Colby had accepted his point of view wholeheartedly, but he also was a practical man. He'd just make sure she never got another chance to run amok.

They talked quietly for a long time, filling in some of the gaps in each other's knowledge. He told her of his family, she of hers. When the fire was embers and the night stars fully out, he realized that she was drooping with weariness. He shifted her gently and felt her grunt as her sore muscles protested.

"Really sore, darling?" he asked compassionately.

"Really sore," she admitted.

He laughed ruefully. "Oh, well, I suppose a small

amount of patience won't hurt me too badly. You've got until the day after tomorrow, darling Colby, to get over being saddle sore, so I advise you to set your mind to a quick recovery."

"The day after tomorrow?" repeated Colby obediently, and then more alertly, "Why only until the day after tomorrow?"

"Because by the time we get back to the ranch, your parents and my parents should have arrived for our wedding, which will take place the following day. While you were haring over the countryside, I was making phone calls, arranging it all. And by the way, Lieutenant Mac-Guire sends his best regards."

"What!"

Jase's voice could only be described as smug. "I called him and told him you were unofficially resigning your unofficial job because your husband-to-be has a thing about having a working wife. He congratulated me on finding the perfect solution for his problem and my own."

"And what were those problems?" Colby asked dangerously.

"Well, I need immunity from prosecution on a kidnapping charge, and what better way to get it than to marry the kidnappee? And MacGuire was worried about your safety, you know. He wants to close the club, but not at the cost of your life."

Jase's voice had gone decidedly grim. He had had a most informative talk with Lt. MacGuire. Colby was a lovely nitwit, both men agreed, to have taken such a risk. Matt MacGuire was not such a bad fellow after all. He was honestly glad to have Colby safely out of the whole dirty mess. Jase could forgive him quite a bit now, since he had Colby here in his arms, and here she'd stay.

The lovely nitwit wiggled wrathfully in his arms. "You —you high-handed, arrogant, dictatorial beast! You . . ." The rest of her words were smothered beneath his seeking mouth.

When he let her breathe again, he warned her, "If you're not so sore that you can still fight, then you're not so sore that I can't make love to you."

"Are we quarreling, Jase darling?" Colby's voice was husky and just a trifle breathless.

"Yes, I suppose you could say we are," he answered reflectively.

"Good," Colby stated with satisfaction. "That means we can make up in the proper way for all lovers to end their quarrels." She pulled his head back down to hers and forgot all about her aches and pains.

Colby might have been stiff and sore from her hours on horseback, but it didn't seem to measurably affect the sensual fluidity of her body as she fitted her curved contours smoothly against Jase. This time there would be no interruptions, no lurking specter of Margy and her frying pan.

"Colby?" Jase questioned her softly.

"I love you, Jase," she answered simply.

Without another word he rolled away from her, stood up, and pulled her to her feet. With deft motions he spread and smoothed the sleeping bag to make a pallet for their pleasure.

Colby used the toe of one shoe to pull down the heel of its fellow and then repeated the process with the other foot. Her socks were no problem, since she hadn't resumed them after her session at streamside, but then she stood irresolute for a moment, suddenly shy.

Jase was smoothing the sleeping bag, half turned away

182

from her, and the illusory sense of privacy restored her momentarily lost composure. With steady fingers she unsnapped the waist of her jeans and slid the zipper down with a soft hiss of metal. With graceful, natural ease she stepped out of her jeans and folded them neatly, placing them and her shoes by the piled saddles.

She turned back to find Jase, already stripped of his shirt and boots, standing at one corner of the spread-out sleeping bag, obviously appreciating the glimmering length of her legs showing from beneath her free-hanging shirt. The moon was bright enough to show his expression clearly, but Colby hoped that it wasn't bright enough to show the red flush she could feel running beneath the skin of her face and neck. Later there would be the ease of intimacy, but this first time . . .

Jase sensed or saw, for as her hands went fumblingly to the first button of her shirt, he stepped forward and stayed them. "Let me," he said huskily. "Let me, my princess of the night."

Colby stood quietly as he undid her shirt and pushed it off her shoulders and down her arms. He tossed it aside and his hands went to the snap of her bra. With a flicker of humor Colby noted that he was no expert when it came to the intricacies of the fastenings of a woman's underclothes. The knowledge was oddly reassuring. When he pulled the wisp of lace away, baring her upper body completely, she stood proudly before him, content to let him look his fill.

His breath rasped harshly in his throat and he pulled her strongly into his arms. The skin of his chest was furrily warm against the bared, tender skin of her breasts, which flattened against him as he pressed her close. His hands ran warmly up and down the length of her spine and cupped the curve of her buttocks, pulling her firmly against the urgent thrust of his hard body.

Kisses and broken bits of endearments were scattered over her cheeks and neck while he lowered her to the waiting pallet and, after removing the final, frail barrier of her silken briefs and the more sturdy barrier of his own jeans, he began the slow and thorough possession of her body with his own.

With care and tender concern he explored the mystery of the difference between the hard solidity of his masculine frame and the soft, yielding pliancy of her own. His fingers learned her body, from the already familiar soft rise of her breasts, tipped with the achingly hard buds of her nipples, to the deep warm recesses, secret no longer beneath the invasion of his desire.

The words he whispered invaded her mind as surely as his body penetrated hers and she was worshiped with his mouth and his mind while his hands shaped her to his requirements.

He prepared her, he persuaded her, and when the moment of sharp intrusion came, he soothed the inevitable swift pang and patiently restoked to blazing heat the passion that had been chilled by the necessary rending pain. Her cry of surprised satisfaction echoed with his own deep groan of pleasure over the empty land.

It was pagan to lie naked in love beneath the stars, but for Colby, the hard ground beneath her and the night breeze against her sensitized skin added an extra dimension of sensuality to her rites of initiation in Jase's powerful arms.

When they finally lay spent and satiated, her head on his shoulder, his thigh thrown over her legs to keep her close to the length of his relaxed body, she murmured drowsily, "The world is empty, save for thee and me. No need have we for aught, or for other company."

"A quote?" Jase questioned softly, nuzzling into the cloud of scented dark hair pillowed so comfortably on his shoulder.

"No," she chuckled quietly. "Just spur-of-the-moment bad poetry."

Her hand traced lazily up and down the ridges of muscle covering his ribs, drifted down past his waist to the lean side of his hip. He held her closer but did not impede the subtle exploration of her hand. As he now knew her body, she would learn of his, in her own time, in her own way.

Her fingers tiptoed back up, through the dark hair on his chest, onto the side of his neck, to flatten into a caressing palm that molded itself lovingly along his cheek. Her thumb traced over his lips and they captured and kissed the pad of her thumb as it swept across slowly. As he kissed that exploring finger he opened his mouth slightly and Colby felt the warm tip of his tongue tentatively taste the flavor of her skin again. She shivered with remembered rapture that tongue tip's foray, evocative of the recent forays it had made so deliciously over other parts of her skin.

Jase swept out a long arm and drew the sleeping bag's extra width up over them, enclosing them in a cocoon of warmth. With a small amount of contortion he managed to zip the bag closed around them. It was a close, intimate fit. Jase turned Colby over until she lay against him, her back nestled into his chest, his thighs tucked up beneath the backs of her legs.

Colby said "Jase" drawlingly.

"Hmmm?" He cupped a warm hand around her breast.

185

"You only brought one sleeping bag."

"Obviously." She could hear the smile in his voice.

"Didn't you expect to catch up with me?"

"Of course."

"Well?" she insisted.

"I knew we'd only need one," he said with smug finality.

"How nice to be omniscient," she murmured.

"Even nicer to sleep with you in my arms," he retorted, and effectively closed the subject. Colby was fair-minded and there was no way she could argue about that. Jase might have kidnapped her initially, but now she was a willing captive of his love.